By Stacey R. Campbell

with illustrations by
M. S. Corley

green darner PRESS

green darner PRESS

Published by Green Darner Press
9600 Stone Avenue North
Seattle, Washington 98103

Green Darner Press is an imprint of Gemelli Press LLC

Cover design and illustrations by M. S. Corley
Typesetting by Enterline Design Services LLC

Paperback ISBN: 978-0-9884784-4-2
Hardback ISBN: 978-0-9884784-9-7
Library of Congress Control Number: 2014955892

To my father, Jon Runstad,
who filled my head with stories about a boy and a mouse
&
To my husband, Donald,
who finally told me to "sit down and write!"

I love you.

REVIEWS

"I liked this book a lot! It was action packed. Shiver me timbers, it has even made me want to be a pirate for Halloween." —Madelin, age 8

"The story made me smile. It›s just a fun book to read. —Isabella D., age 10 3/4

"I would recommend this book to kids who like great action and fun characters." —Landen I., age 9

"A thrilling adventure on the high seas. I want a talking mouse as a BFF!" —Macia M., age 12

"I think it›s a really good, interesting story. I like the characters, especially Christopher and Leo."
—Peter R., age 10

"I liked this book because I never knew what was going to happen next which made it really exciting to read!"
—Anders W., age 11

"This book has loads of adventure and gave us good dreams. A boy hero, stolen treasure, awful pirates, the royal navy, a talking mouse, a helpful monkey, good friends and the call of the sea...buy this book or walk the plank! ARRGH!!!!" —Cole and Ellery P., age 7

"I love this book. I think I›ll read it again. An exiting adventure." —Ellen N., age 11

"I would recommend this book to kids who like big adventures on the sea." —Branko J., age 11

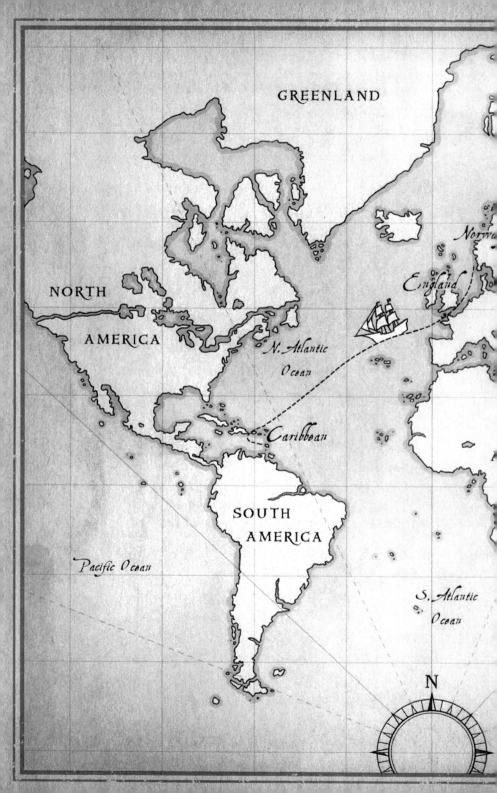

Arctic Sea

ASIA

EUROPE

Pacific Ocean

Indian Ocean

AUSTRALIA

GLOSSARY OF TERMS

Aft	The rear or back end of a ship.
Bilge	The lowest level of the ship, typically wet, often full of rodents.
Doubloons	Gold coins, Spanish in origin.
Forecastle	The forward part of the ship below decks; traditionally used as the crew's living quarters.
Fore Hatch	Forward hatch or opening leading down into the lower levels of the ship.
Gangplank	A moveable plank used as a ramp to board or disembark from a ship or boat.
Gunwales	The upper edge of the side of a boat or ship.
Halyard	The rope used for raising and lowering a sail.
Holly stone	Porous brick used to scrub dirt off of the decks of a ship.
Hull	The main body of a ship.
Jib	A triangular sail set forward of the foremost mast.
Lee	The opposite or sheltered side of a ship, away from the wind.

Mess   The area of the ship in which the crew eats their meals.

Midshipman Lower most ranking officer on a British ship, roughly equivalent to a present day petty officer in rank and responsibilities.

Mizzenmast The mast aft located behind the ship's main mast.

Pallet   A portable platform on which goods can be moved, stacked, or stored; also, a crude or makeshift bed.

Port   The nautical term for left (opposite of starboard/right).

Quadrant   A historical instrument used for taking nautical measurements.

Ratlines   A series of small ropes fastened across a sailing ship's shrouds like rungs of a ladder, used for climbing the rigging.

Rigging   The system of ropes or cables employed to support a ship's masts.

Rudder   A flat piece of wood or metal hinged vertically near the stern of the boat for steering.

Shrouds   A set of ropes forming part of the standing rigging of a sailing vessel, which supports the mast from the sides.

Sextant   An instrument used for measuring the angular distance between objects.

Sloop   A one-masted sailboat with a fore-and-aft main sail and a jib.

A small square-rigged sailing warship with two or three masts.

Starboard   The nautical term for right (opposite of port/left).

Stern   The rearmost part of a ship or boat.

Tiller   A horizontal bar fitted to the head of a boat's rudder and used as a lever for steering.

Topgallant   The uppermost section of a square-rigged sailing ship's mast.

Topside   The uppermost part of the ship above the waterline.

Transom   The flat surface forming the stern of a vessel or a horizontal beam reinforcing the stern of a vessel.

The toppling roller at the harbor mouth
Are spattering the bows with foam,
And the anchor's catted, and she's heading for the south
With her topsails sheeted for home –
The Buccaneer – John Masefield

CHAPTER 1

Riiiiiiiiip.

Christopher winced as his pants caught on something when he tried to move. He looked down to see the tip of a rusty nail digging into his calf. A lone boy hanging around the docks shouldn't draw too much attention, he thought. Besides, it might be the best place to find a ride away from the city and the workhouse that had been his prison for the last eight months.

The Norphan Home for Wayward Boys was not a place one wanted to stay for long. Father Svenn, the master of the house, used the boys to produce his famed pickled herring, a small silver fish preserved in a sour brine that made Christopher sick. Father Svenn cared little about his charges' well-being, only about his product's bottom line.

The elders in his village had sent Christopher to the orphanage after his parents had disappeared, assuming they were dead. Christopher never saw their bodies, though, so he wasn't so sure. The evidence didn't seem to add up, but he was only twelve years old at the time and adults rarely listen to children when they think they are being controversial. The elders took his father's farm, leaving Christopher with no money and no place to call home, and so it was to Norphan's he was sent.

The discarded wooden pallet where he lay was hidden behind rubbish in an abandoned alley not far from a dozen different ships heading in the direction he wished to travel. Merchants called their wares from the busy street in front of the alley as horses trotted past pulling carriages. A window on the other side of the lane flew open and a woman flipped a dusty floor mat into the air. Behind him on top of a mound of molding fishnets, a fat street cat sat contentedly, cleaning his paws.

Christopher's mother had once talked about an uncle that lived in London. He hoped to find him now, exchanging hard work for passage across the northern sea.

Christopher yawned, wondering when was the best time to approach the captains of the ships to inquire about a position. He ran his hand down his face grimacing at the smell of fish on his hands. Hiding in a barrel of herring seemed like a brilliant idea at the time. He shouldn't complain though. It worked.

"Fresh bread!" a man from a nearby store yelled. Christopher's empty stomach growled. A small silver fish slipped from the cuff of his coat and fell to the ground. The cat, still perched on the discarded nets, cocked his head. Christopher's pale blue eyes stung from pickling

juices and his sandy blond hair refused to unstick from his pale cheeks. What else was hidden between the folds of his clothes he wondered?

Two men turned into the alley.

"Stinky!" the taller of the two hissed. "Ye be listening to me or not?"

Christopher peered between the planks of the sour-smelling barrel skeletons he was tucked behind to see boots, shiny black boots, sparkling in the wedge of sunlight that cascaded down the deserted cobbled lane. Fear prickled down his spine as he recognized the tip of a saber peaking out from beneath the man's heavy blue coat.

"I heard ye." The second man said, shoving a warm sticky bun between rotting teeth.

Boots growled. A jagged scar stretched from his chin to his eye, paralyzing the lid so that it no longer closed. Sweat pooled on his brow. He hated having to repeat things over again.

"Listen ye dolt. Me plan is bulletproof. If the information One Eye obtained be true, the guns Red Blade be want'n be loaded onboard the *Georgiana* in the next port she lay. The Captain of the ship don't even know it yet. All we have to do is give word to our brethren once them guns be loaded and stay with the ship until Red Blade shows."

Stinky adjusted his tricon cap then wiped the crumbs from breakfast down the front of his shirt.

Boots put his hands on his hips and raised his chin to the sky. "This be the chance we be waiting for, matey. A way to show Red Blade what we're made of. Perhaps even earn'n a ship of our own."

A second cat that had been perched on top of an abandoned cask vaulted onto the pallet next to Christopher. "Meow," the feline said and then began to purr while eating the small silver fish that had fallen from his cuff. The cat on top of the nets lowered his head and leapt down to join his friend. A fish float crashed to the cobbles.

The pirates stilled.

"Shoo," Christopher whispered, pushing the cats away. He stripped off his fish-riddled coat and crawled to the next pallet as a third cat wandered their way. A hissing battle commenced.

The crate hiding Christopher shifted. "And what do we have here?" The man in the boots sneered.

Christopher turned, but the words he wanted to speak lodged in his throat as the blade of a saber brushed the side of his face.

"I asked ye a question, boy. I expect ye to be answer'n."

Christopher choked, but still no words came.

"Cat got yer tongue?" asked the thin giant's friend. Stinky was shorter by a head, rounder by half, and covered in filth. Earrings dangled from both sides of his head and a long waxed mustache spun to his ears.

"Kill 'em!" Boots ordered. "He done heard what we said."

Christopher's eyes widened as the round man cocked his pistol.

A group of children ran across the start of the lane. "Your work is not done! Come back here!" their mother yelled.

"Wait," Boots said, raising his hand. "I got me an idea." He stroked his chin. "A healthy young boy could be useful, if not worth somethin' when we reach the Caribbean. Two bags of gold at very least."

"He's thin," Stinky snorted.

"He'll grow."

"But what happens if he opens his yap?" Stinky asked, bringing the butt of his pistol down on Christopher's head. Christopher crumbled to the ground. Stinky placed his pistol back into the scarlet sash tied around his waist.

Boots shrugged. "We'll cut out his tongue."

CHAPTER 2

Christopher slowly became aware of his body as he regained consciousness.

"Both arms, two legs…" Christopher said through a shiver. He was wet but nothing was sticky to the touch, so he figured it was just water, not his own blood.

"Oh," he moaned, feeling the enormous bump on the side of his head. "Where am I?"

He could feel a wall in front of him and slowly dragged his bruised body over so that he could lean against it.

A few meager rays of light managed to sneak between the thick boards above Christopher's head allowing him to see the outlines of his confines. Crates stacked high next to barrels reached the room's low ceiling. Gathered ropes hung from rafters and unfamiliar sounds echoed throughout the dark chamber where he sat.

"Ugh . . . ," he mumbled, inhaling the overwhelming stench of mildew. His body swayed from side to side as the room rocked back and forth. He was on a boat. The realization took his breath away.

"No!" Christopher pounded his fist against the floor.

"This can't be happening to me!" He reached forward trying to stand, but the throbbing pain in his head made him dizzy.

He took a deep breath and rolled to his knees. Spotting a hatch on the ceiling across the room, he decided to crawl through the maze of unidentified cargo until he sat beneath the portal.

"Help!" Christopher screamed climbing the rungs of the ladder. The locked door refused to budge.

Something scurried by in the darkness below.

The light peaking through the planks above his head started to fade. Before the last glimmer of light disappeared, Christopher crawled back to the spot he had started from.

He woke to the sound of heavy footsteps. The boys at the orphanage told stories of pirates like the ones who had kidnapped him. None of them ended happily.

"Where's that lantern?"

"Can ye see him?"

"No, ye dolt! Bring me the light!"

Christopher peered through heavy lids at the pair of black polished boots making their way down the ladder.

"Is he awake yet?"

"No," Boots snapped, nudging Christopher's still body with his toe.

A small mouse darted across the floor.

"Egad!" Boots yelled jumping.

"What?" Stinky shouted, unsheathing his knife and leaping beside his mate.

"Rat!"

"That ain't no rat, Boots," Stinky said, watching a tail disappear beneath the crate next to the hatch. "That there be a wee mouse."

"I don't care what ye say. The devil be after me!"

Stinky clucked his tongue and kneeled to see where the mouse hid. "Them be good eat'n if I canna catch him."

"I don't care what he be. If it be small and crawls, I don't like it!"

CHAPTER 3

Christopher drifted in and out of sleep to the sound of Boots' mouse scurrying across the floor. He didn't care if he was there since it meant he was not alone. In fact the thought of a furry companion strangely comforted him. The ship moved with the waves, moaning as it rolled over one crest then surfed down the face of the next.

As the sun rose higher in the sky, the small storage hold where Christopher sat grew brighter. He pulled himself against the wall sitting so that his back rested against the wooden planks of the hull. His head throbbed, and he couldn't remember the last time he ate—two, maybe three days? How long had he been asleep?

The scurrying sound stopped. Christopher peered hazily to see if he could catch a glimpse at his new fuzzy friend. From across the room the mouse emerged, a worn leather bag clutched in his teeth. When the mouse was mere feet from him, it stopped, stood on its hind legs, and walked upright around to the front of the satchel. Christopher shook his head not believing his eyes. The mouse opened the bag and an apple rolled out.

Christopher rubbed his eyes. The mouse nudged the fruit toward him. Again the mouse crawled into the bag, this time emerging with a crust of bread. Christopher inhaled. His stomach grumbled.

The mouse cocked his head. "There's cheese in there too," he said.

Christopher's eyes rolled back and he slid to the floor.

When he woke again the food was still there. Christopher poked at the bread. It looked real. He picked it up. It smelled real. Christopher took a bite.

Next he reached for the apple. The sweet juices exploded in his mouth. If he were dreaming he did not want to wake. Finally he reached for the bag and pulled out a wedge of cheese. When he put the bag back down on the floor, the mouse was there.

"Told you," the mouse said, shrugging his furry shoulders.

Christopher's food caught in the back of throat and he gagged. Pounding his fist to his chest, he caught his breath.

"Hello?" Christopher poked the tiny brown figure with his finger.

"Ouch!"

"Am I dead?" Christopher said.

"No. Besides that nasty welt on your head, you are perfectly healthy," the mouse replied.

Christopher's jaw dropped.

"You are not crazy either, but I can understand your surprise. Most humans react this way when they meet one of my kind. My name is Leonardo Mousekins, human guide number 1167, at your service. But my friends call me Leo," he said, bowing deeply.

Christopher stared.

"I am a teacher of sorts, a protector, and a friend if you choose." Leo said, extending his paw. "It's nice to meet you."

Christopher eyed the mouse, then took the paw between his thumb and index finger.

"If you lift me up so I might be able to look you in the eye, I will explain things to you more thoroughly."

Christopher took a deep breath and laid his hand down on the ground. The mouse's tiny paws tickled his calloused palm. Christopher had only seen field mice running around the barn back at home. He had never actually held one or seen one up close. That this one was talking to him was beyond belief.

"Don't be scared. I won't bite . . . at least I won't bite you." The mouse grinned, his whiskers twitching from side to side.

Leo let Christopher finish eating before he continued.

"Interspecies communication is not an easy thing to do," Leo said. "It takes years of schooling to master and to become a human guide. In fact, very few animals have the intellectual qualifications it takes to pass the rigorous training." Leo tapped his head to emphasize his point. "Working with humans has been my dream for as long as I can remember," he said. "My father was an attack mouse before me and his father before that. It's what they called us back then."

Christopher nodded, not quite believing what he saw.

"I was at the top of my class—graduated with honors," Leo said, puffing out his chest. "Human guiding is one of the most respected professions in the animal kingdom. There are hundreds of us scattered all over the world. Since graduating from HGU, Human Guide University, I've been trying to find someone like you."

Leo pointed to Christopher then began to pace, wringing his paws together as he walked from one side of Christopher's palm to the other.

"Originally, human guides weren't guides at all; we were bodyguards who protected the innocent, which is where the name 'attack animals' came from. We were trained in the physical forms of fighting—karate, kung fu, swordsmanship, you name it. But when guides did nothing but fight for our humans, our humans became lazy. They lost their ability to help themselves.

"That's when the Human Guide Council decided to switch from protector to teacher. The human brain is an amazing instrument. The council found that if a human is taught to believe in himself or herself and have knowledge of their surroundings, their weaknesses turn into strengths, leaving them virtually unstoppable.

"Oh, I can still fight," Leo assured him, throwing his paws into the air at an imaginary foe. "But my superiors discourage it."

Christopher wanted to laugh but simply smirked. Leo looked more like something one might step on than an Attack Mouse For-Hire.

CHAPTER 4

When he woke up the next morning, Christopher found another apple, two pieces of smoked meat, and a cup of water on the floor in front of him. Leo sat with crossed legs beside the food.

Any thought that Leo had been a figment of Christopher's imagination brought on by hunger rushed from his head when he recalled all that he had learned the night before.

"I can't believe this is real," Christopher said, still in awe.

Leo grinned so that his front teeth showed beneath his pink nose. His bulbous black eyes twinkled. "You will."

Christopher cleared the sleep from the corner of his eyes. "So what do we do now?"

"Take inventory."

"Pardon me?"

"Lesson One: Know your surroundings. Look around and really see where you are, using all your senses."

Christopher rolled his eyes.

"No use me telling you. It is always better to find out yourself."

"Okay," Christopher agreed, picking up the apple.

As the hours passed, their friendship developed. Christopher told Leo about how he had lost his parents, the Norphan Home for Wayward Boys, and finally about the two men who had kidnapped him.

"Pirates," Leo grumbled. "Of all the men who sail the Seven Seas, those who take what doesn't belong to them are by far the worst."

Surprisingly, Boots and Stinky only came down to check on Christopher once more during their trip to England. He feigned sleep again and was saved from further inspection by Leo, who wove through Boots' feet, expertly avoiding Stinky's attempts at capture with ease.

On the fourth day, the familiar sounds and movement Christopher had finally gotten used to stopped. The ship slowed and Christopher could hear the moan of the halyards being eased.

"The sails are being taken in," Leo said excitedly, jumping from Christopher's lap.

The two new friends, boy and mouse, sat side by side as the ship sailed into the harbor. After a little while the groaning stopped and the ship stilled. Finally, Leo's nose twitched. His right ear stood at attention. "Are you ready?" he asked, hearing the two men approach.

Christopher swallowed. "Yes."

"Then I'm going topside to see where we are."

CHAPTER 5

The hatch separating Christopher from the outside world opened. The storage hold flooded with light.

Christopher leaned against the inner hull as Boots climbed down the ladder.

"Yer awake," the pirate jeered, scanning the room with his one good eye for sign of vermin. "Fair'n well I see."

Christopher fidgeted with the frayed end of his shirt.

"Don't be try'n noth'n," Boots warned, grabbing the boy's arm. Christopher took a shaky breath. The pirate dragged him toward the hatch. "Listen closely, lad, 'cause this is how things go'n work. First ye go'n to tell me yer name."

Christopher winced as Boot's grip tightened. "Christopher," he said quietly.

"Second, there'll be no talk'n."

Stinky stood on deck watching for the crew's return. "Hurry up, Boots!" he warned.

"Third, do as I say and ye live. Step out of line, and ye die."

Christopher nodded.

"Is the coast clear?" Boots hollered.

"Aye!"

Boots pushed Christopher up the ladder. "I'm tell'n the Captain of this rat barge yer me nephew and be mute. Don't even think about make'n friends. No mix'n with the crew."

It took a minute for Christopher's eyes to adjust to the daylight. To his left lay the harbor, much bigger than any he had seen before. To his right was a large city.

Christopher's father had taught him about ships. He knew that the masts were the large upright poles that towered into the sky holding the yards. The yards looked like giant arms extending out of the mast and were often referred to as yardarms for just that reason. The rob bands held the sails to the yards. The sails were gathered and tied to the yards when the ship wasn't sailing. Halyards were used to hoist the yards up and down the mast so that the sails could catch the wind, pushing the boat forward. Then long lines called sheets were fastened to the bottom corners of the sails. By pulling on one sheet or the other, the captain and crew were able to sail the boat. On bigger ships, such as the one he stood on now, both the forward, or fore, and main, or mizzen, mast had platforms on them called lookouts. Sailors would climb up onto the lookouts to adjust the sails, look for land, or spot other ships while out at sea.

"From a lookout," Christopher's dad had told him, "you can see forever."

CHAPTER 6

The crew returned to the ship, calling out greetings as they hauled their goods aboard.

As Christopher reached the middle of the ship, he noticed a ramp leading to the dock. His heart rate quickened. He had already escaped from the Norphan Home for Wayward Boys. Could he do it again? He wondered where they were. If he had had the means, he would have slept in a private room, never been in the alley, and purchased passage on such a ship instead of being thrown into a damp holding cell. Boots tensed, sensing the boy's thoughts, and tightened his grip on Christopher's arm. He motioned to the dagger at his waist.

"Be just as easy to slit your throat now if ye be try'n anyth'n. All I have to say is I caught ye thiev'n."

A man, similar in age to Christopher's late father, stood at the bottom of the ramp. He wore a tailored navy coat over a clean, white shirt with grey tailored pants and proper, buckled leather shoes. His greying brown hair was neatly tied back with a thin black ribbon that fluttered in the breeze. He addressed each sailor by name as they bound up the ramp.

"Okay, men," he called. "Once the Georgiana is loaded and her supplies stowed, you may have your leave. Be back by sun up. We sail with the tide."

The crew cheered.

As the last of the sailors boarded the ship, the man giving the orders below stepped onto the plank. He must be the Captain, Christopher thought. A girl who looked his age stood at the Captain's side. The girl's long chestnut hair curled past her shoulders, tickling her cheeks as it caught in the wind. She couldn't have been much taller than Christopher, who had always been short for his age, but unlike him, her cheeks were full and stained red from the sun. She reached for the Captain's hand and together they boarded the ship. Christopher's breath caught in the back of his throat. He had no idea the Captain would have his daughter onboard.

Boots pushed Christopher forward.

"Good afternoon, Mr. Jones," the Captain welcomed. "Are we loaded and well?"

"In the process, sir."

The Captain's hazel eyes took in the boy to his midshipman's right. "And what do we have here?"

Boots prodded Christopher forward, stepping in closely behind. The marauder unsheathed his dagger secretly so that no one could see him pressing its tip into the small of Christopher's back.

Christopher scanned the deck for Leo.

Breathe, he told himself. Boots pushed the dagger further into Christopher's back, and Christopher felt the cold steel blade piercing his skin. A small trickle of blood ran down his spine.

"Well, sir, I've run into a bit of a family situation," Boots said in voice laced with a sugary sweetness that Christopher knew was fake. "My dear sister, bless her care'n heart, has just now brought me this fine young man. He's my nephew, Christopher." Boots smiled, his tongue pressing through a gap left by a missing lower tooth . "The problem, sir, is that he can't speak. Never has. My sister is awful concerned 'bout him learn'n a useful trade since he can't say a word. She don't want him be'n a burden on anyone once he's grown." Boots looked up at the Captain feigning a worried sigh. " So, I . . . we . . . was wonder'n if the boy could join me here, on the Georgiana?"

"Where is your sister, Mr. Jones?" The Captain asked. "And why isn't she here to ask me herself?"

He thought for a moment, then replied. "The dear woman is heavy with child, sir. I felt it safest to leave her on shore."

Boots thrust Christopher forward, quickly tucking the dagger beneath his shirt. Christopher looked at the

Captain, then to the girl standing beside him and bowed. As he straightened back up he met the girl's chocolate gaze.

"I will train him myself," Boots continued. "And he can share my cabin. I'll make sure he be in no one's way, sir."

"Has he any experience on the high sea?" the Captain inquired.

"No, but he be a strong boy and a hard worker."

The girl tapped her father's shoulder and the Captain turned and leaned down so she could whisper in his ear.

"Well," the Captain said with a smile, "it seems my daughter thinks the boy would make a good addition to the crew." The girl's cheeks turned pink, and she ducked her head so that Christopher could not see her face. "She has asked that I consider your proposition. She has been surrounded by sailors, most of them twice her age thus far on the trip. It would be nice to have someone similar in years onboard. I won't be able to pay him, but he may join us. Teach him what he needs to know."

"Thank you, Cap'n," Boots replied, grinning.

"Son," the Captain said, "I am Captain Malcolm Hughes and this is my youngest daughter, Lucy. I run a tight ship. Associate yourself with the onboard rules. We shall see if you can earn your keep."

Christopher bowed.

The Captain nodded. "With that settled," he said, turning to Lucy, "I must be off. I have a meeting with the head of the port. I'll be back soon, then I shall take you to see London." Lucy obediently moved toward a beautifully hand-carved mahogany door at the stern of the boat.

Christopher coughed. London! He looked over at the wharf wondering in which part of city his uncle lived.

Lucy turned just before reaching her cabin and looked at the boy. His light blue eyes found hers. This time she smiled.

Captain Hughes straightened his coat, placed the hat clutched in his hand on his head, and bid his crew farewell.

CHAPTER 7

Soft afternoon light flooded the cabin from the large aft portholes lining the transom of the ship. Lucy attempted to brush a speck of dirt from her skirt but shrugged when it refused to leave the fabric.

In her mind she went over the new boy's face. Strong jaw, honest eyes. Her mother would approve of his looks. He smelled a bit like low tide, though, and desperately in need of a bath.

"Oh well," she sighed, sinking into the leather reading chair in her father's lounge. At least the long sail across the Atlantic wouldn't be quite so boring now that there was someone else around her age onboard. Even if he couldn't speak, he could listen. She didn't mind doing the talking for them both.

The only other sailors even close to her age were a set of twins who worked up in the rigging with Mr. Bruce, one of her father's senior crewmen. They were nice enough boys, but they were over five years older than Lucy, and she found they didn't have much to talk about.

In fact the only other person Lucy talked with, besides

her father's shipboard officers, was the Georgiana's cook, a dear family friend her father had conned into sailing with him because, according to her father, "There is no finer chef in all of the Caribbean."

Lucy pursed her lips and blew the hair from her face. She liked the way the new boy did not look away when she glanced at him like most boys her age did. They weren't used to her frankness. Her father told her it wasn't polite to stare, but she didn't care. At home on the island of Antigua, no one really worried about manners, unless Lord Nelson was in town.

It wasn't until she turned fifteen that she would have to behave like a proper lady. She'd already seen her sisters conform to society's rules once they came of age, but at nearly thirteen she was still allowed to do as she pleased.

Her thoughts went back to Christopher and her good fortune that he was aboard. Evelyn, Lucy's oldest sister, had sailed to Africa with father; they saw elephants. Elizabeth, her next eldest sister, had gone to France; they had seen castles.

Now, to Lucy, with someone her own age joining them, England didn't seem quite as dull.

CHAPTER 8

"Ha," Boots mumbled as he turned away from the Captain, "me plan is working."

Crewmen hurried in and out of open hatches carrying supplies for the journey ahead.

"Excuse me," one said pushing Christopher aside as he made his way through the busy maze of activity.

Boots ducked through the main fore hatch, entering the ship. "This way," he growled.

They came to a steep set of narrow stairs and waited for several of the crew to move out of the way so they could descend.

Several large shipboard guns lined the sides of the next open room. Sailors lashed water barrels to the sturdy support beams that held up the thick wooden grating above their heads. The grating opened up to the deck above, letting in light. Christopher could see where he had stood only moments before.

One crewman stacked iron shot, what cannonballs on a ship are called, into neatly secured piles. Christopher noticed that each gun was positioned in front of a small door in the ship's hull that could be opened when the guns were being fired.

After leaving the gun deck, they walked through a series of hallways. Christopher saw what he thought was a makeshift hospital with two berths and who must have been the ship's doctor going over various medical supplies. Several other doors led to even smaller rooms. Above these rooms were signs listing the various titles the occupants held.

Again, Christopher was forced down a series of steep wooden steps. The portholes that let fresh air into the boat no longer existed on this level.

The next room they entered looked like a kitchen, or as it is referred to on a ship, a galley. An elderly man with a bulging belly balanced a crate of apples on his hip. His shiny, bald head reflected the light of the lantern hanging from the ceiling. Vegetables, grains, dried meats, and other such cooking provisions were piled on the counters before him.

"Afternoon," the man called seeing Boots, Stinky, and the boy. "And what have we here? Another mouth to feed?"

"This be me nephew, Christopher," Boots snarled. "He be join'n us for the cross'n."

Christopher held out his hand for the man to shake, but Boots pulled him away before they could make contact.

"I'm Cookie," the man said.

A large brick oven with a massive metal pot hanging from a cast iron arm stood at the side of the room and an array of pots swung from the ceiling.

A miniature monkey with an off-white face jumped on Cookie's shoulder from the shelving above.

"Hello, Sugar girl," Cookie cooed, scratching the fluff of brown behind the monkey's ear. Sugar flashed Christopher a toothy primate grin. "Looks like Miss Lucy's been playing dress up with you again." Cookie reached for the pale pink bow tied around her neck, but Sugar swatted his hand away.

"Eep," said Sugar.

"Sugar here is a wee capuchin monkey who smuggled herself aboard the ship when we were picking up sugar cane on the island of Nevis several years ago."

Forgetting about Boots, Christopher reached for the monkey.

"Off with ye, old man," Boots barked, slapping Christopher's hand away. "The boy be here to learn a useful trade, not to play with yer stupid pet!"

Sugar hissed.

Boots pushed Christopher forward and down an unlit corridor, just off the crew's mess. "In here," Boots growled, opening the door.

CHAPTER 9

Boots and Stinky scoured the area surrounding the Port Office after locking Christopher in the cabin.

"There," Boots waved, pointing to the deserted lane to the left of the office's entrance.

"But what about them soldiers?" Stinky said, gesturing to the two-armed guards standing watch outside the main entrance.

Boot's eye settled on a young woman walking toward them down the busy sidewalk. "That'll do the trick," he sneered, letting the end of his jagged scar pull at corner of his steel grey eye.

Boots crossed the street, matching his stride to hers. When the woman passed the guards, Boots pushed her into an oncoming carriage. The driver cursed, the woman screamed, and the two guards abandoned their posts.

"Bloody good show," Stinky chortled as they darted down the lane.

To the good fortune of the pirates, the windows were open in the office where Captain Hughes met with Lord

Wilson, the head of the merchant line, and the Commander of the Royal Navy.

"The winds be on our side today," Stinky snorted.

Boots elbowed his mate in the gut and raised a crooked finger to his lips. "Shh . . . "

"We would like the guns to be placed on your boat, Captain Hughes," the Commander stated. "I will give you a letter of safe passage, and upon arrival you will be well compensated."

"I understand what you are asking, sir," Captain Hughes replied. "But I am the Captain of a merchant vessel, not a navy ship. The waters you are asking me to sail through are notoriously dangerous. Tortola is known to be a lawless island. Most of the area is overcome by chaos. I am undermanned and underarmed. If word of this were to leak, it would be very difficult to defend my ship against aggressors."

"Captain, may I remind you, we have already taken all this into account? That is why we are taking such great precautions to keep this mission under wraps," Lord Wilson replied.

"No one will expect a merchant vessel of such little influence to be carrying guns for the King," the commander of the Royal Navy declared. "Besides there is no other option. Our ships are occupied with the Americas at present. The refortification of our territories in the southern seas is critical to the effort."

"The guns will be loaded tonight under the cover of darkness," Lord Wilson instructed. "They will be in unmarked crates and loaded by plain clothed soldiers. We will replace the cargo you have now and send it through on the next ship. I shall even put one of my best men, Admiral Cunningham, onboard with you so he may advise you during the voyage."

The idea of having a stranger of such rank join his crew made Captain Hughes wince. Arrangements would need to be made. One of his own men would have to give up their cabin.

"You should be quite safe," Lord Wilson assured.

"I have my ship, my crew, and my daughter to think about. I am not comfortable with what you are asking me to do," the Captain pleaded.

The Commander bristled. "Well then, you must make sure word of your cargo does not get out!"

CHAPTER 10

Only the passing gulls and alley rats could see Boots and Stinky as they sat leering at one another outside the Port Office's window. Timing their departure with the distraction caused by the Commander leaving the building, Boots and Stinky emerged from the shadows and rejoined the throngs of people passing by on the crowded street.

"The pirate gods favor us today, Stinky old boy. We must get word to our brothers," said Boots.

"Aye," Stinky replied.

"To the Ram's Head!"

A man the size of an ox stood guard at the front entrance of London's seediest tavern. The foul rank of human waste, rotten food, and spilt drinks burned the nostrils of normal men, but Boots and Stinky inhaled it deeply, relishing the smell at the base of their lungs. This was their kind of place, a home away from home. A thin man with a patched eye pounded on the keys of an untuned piano as a harlot in a corset sang a raunchy sea shanty.

Boots grinned. "This way," he said spotting their mates.

Three shadowed men crowded around the corner table. "The guns be load'n tonight," Boots growled to its occupants. The pirates nodded.

"Sit!" the raider wearing an eye patch ordered. "Have ye come upon this information firsthand?"

"Aye, I have! Heard it with me own ears. The ship is to be load'n this even'n, then make for open waters with the morn'n tide. She's well kept, but old. The course be Tortola." Boots said. "Captain Red Blade and the *Dragon's Breath* should have no problem overtak'n her once she be near."

"Aye," the one-eyed man agreed. "Will a king's officer be onboard?"

"Aye."

"Then the Georgiana will sail through Anagada Channel and that will place her right in our hands."

One of the men referred to by the others as Pickled Pete grabbed for the bottle of rum that sat in the middle of the table. He removed the cork with his teeth and filled the wooden cups sitting empty in front of them.

One Eye raised his glass. "Arrgh," he growled. "To the Dragon's Breath!"

"Arrgh!" The men replied, draining their tankards.

"Snake," One Eye said to the man with a serpent tattoo slithering up his arm. "Get word to our crew that we sail in the morn. We'll meet up with Red Blade and take the

Georgiana by the time she makes landfall."

One Eye smashed his chalice to the table. "Make haste,
Boots. All those who wish to become men of fortune are
welcome to join us."

CHAPTER II

Why did she have to look at him, Christopher wondered as he peered through the murky darkness of his new room.

He was grateful to be alive and out of the dank hole he had been thrown in before. Christopher could just see a lantern hanging over a desk in the corner. Finding a flint in the drawer, he reached for the glass and placed it carefully to the side. After a few attempts at lighting the wick, the flame jumped and illuminated the cabin in a warm orange glow.

A mildew-ridden mattress with a scratchy wool blanket sat on the single bunk against the wall. In the corner opposite sat an old sea trunk secured by an oversized iron lock. Christopher rattled the fastener, but it refused to budge. He sat on the bed and rested his head in hands. Was escape even an option?

"Oh my," Leo squeaked, as he squeezed into the room from underneath the cabin door. "I didn't think those men would ever leave. With all their arguing and whispering, I thought I'd be stuck out there forever. I simply have to find an easier way in here next time." Leo brushed the dirt that clung to his fur then adjusted a red knit cap hat acquired since their last meeting.

"Leo," Christopher said with a smile, happy to see his friend again. "Where have you been?"

"Why, besides a quick look around, I have been with you all day. Just out of sight. I must say I am not very fond of your captors. Is your back all right? Would you like me to take a look at the cut?"

"No, I think it's okay. It's not very deep. Did you see Sugar?"

"Of course." Leo replied. "I told her about you days ago. She's been helping me get you food."

Christopher's jaw dropped. "She's not . . . another guide, is she?"

"Oh no," Leo said shaking his head. "But she is certainly smart enough if she wanted to go through the training. Not much happens onboard that she doesn't know about."

"Can you talk to her?"

"Of course! I took Monkey at school. I have a knack for languages; they're pretty easy for me, really."

"Could you teach me too?"

"I don't think so. Humans can't make the guttural fluxes Monkey requires. I'm teaching her how to understand human languages though. She's a good student, a fast learner; she almost has English mastered. She won't be able to talk to you, but she'll be able to understand you well enough."

Christopher shook his head in disbelief.

"What did you think of the Captain?" Leo asked.

Christopher walked to the other side of the compact cabin. "I like him."

"He is a fine man," Leo said. "One of the best on the high seas. It's a shame he might die."

Christopher stopped walking. "What do you mean?"

"When a ship is taken by pirates, the Captain is either killed or ransomed."

Christopher ran his hand through his still stiff hair. "And what will happen to his daughter, Lucy?"

Leo bowed his head but spoke not a word.

"Oh," Christopher said, his voice catching in the back of his throat.

Christopher paced.

"Would you like to leave now?" Leo asked. " Your captors are well away, and my tail can easily pick the bolt on the cabin door."

Christopher took a deep breath and chewed on his lower lip. He had been thinking about his escape plans since meeting the Captain and Lucy. "Leo, I don't have anywhere to go and not a penny to my name."

"What about your uncle?"

Christopher shook his head. "I have never met the

man. I'm not sure he even exists. And if he does, there's no guarantee that he would take me in. In all manner of speaking, I am homeless," Christopher said and exhaled letting his shoulders slump. He drew his hands into fists. "Plus I don't know if I could live with myself if I left the Captain and Lucy to face Boots and Stinky alone."

"Are you sure?" Leo asked.

Christopher inhaled deeply. "Yes," he said.

A small proud grin pulled up the corner of Leo's whiskers. "Then we will need to find proof that Boots and Stinky are up to no good so that the Captain will believe you when you tell him his midshipman is a fraud."

CHAPTER 12

When he returned from the tavern, Boots was either too drunk or too tired to worry about Christopher's evening activities.

"No funny business on my watch," he mumbled as he relocked the door behind him, barely glancing at the sleeping boy on the floor. He placed the key to the door back around his neck where it hung from a worn leather cord.

Boots flopped onto his bunk and began taking off his treasured namesakes. Gently, he removed one boot, then the other, brushing off the day's dirt before placing them on the floor and lying back to fall asleep. He was snoring loudly before his head hit the bed.

Just a few hours later as the sun rose in the eastern sky, the crew of the Georgiana began to stir.

"Christopher, psst . . . time to rise," Leo whispered.

"What time is it? Is it morning already?" Christopher said as he sat up.

"Yes, it's morning and it's time to wake up," Leo urged. "The morning bells will ring very soon, and you need to be ready. It's your first full day on deck. It is important you make good impression."

Leo held out his paw, offering Christopher a handful of the broken coffee beans that he had taken from the galley.

"Want some?" he asked, sucking on the bittersweet grounds.

Boots lay face up on the bunk, snoring; his paralyzed eye stared up at the ceiling. Beads of crystallized drool coated his cheek.

"Disgusting," Christopher said with a wince.

"He came in about two hours after you fell asleep. He was more interested in his bunk than anything else so I didn't bother waking you," Leo confirmed. "I'm going to go have a look around the ship to see if the guns were put onboard last night. Remember, do as you're told and no talking! I'll come find you up on deck when I'm done."

"Okay," Christopher agreed.

Leo squeezed under the cabin door just as the morning bell rang.

The tide was in their favor just after seven thirty. This meant the waters at the harbor's mouth would be at their back, pushing them forward and allowing for an easy passage.

"Top of the morn'n," Boots snarled.

The crew of the Georgiana rushed about on deck. Men climbed up the fore and aft shrouds to get to the yardarms so that they could start adjusting the sails for release.

Boots spied Stinky talking with another man at the rail as they readied the gangplank to be hoisted. Stinky was a common sailor, so he slept with the rest of the crew in the forecastle, the forwardmost cabin on the ship where sailors hung hammocks in rows and slept for short periods between watches.

"Stinky, come here!" Boots demanded.

"Aye, beautiful morn'n to be sure," said Stinky, grinning through rotting gums. The man to his side gave a curt nod.

"Take the boy," Boots ordered. "Make him useful."

Stinky saluted. "Aye, aye, sir!"

The first few breaths of crisp, clear morning air burned Christopher's lungs. A steady breeze blew through the harbor.

"Such a favorable wind can only be a good omen," Christopher heard a sailor say. "If it keeps up we'll have a quick crossing and be in warm waters before the winter winds set in."

Christopher spotted the Captain on the upper aft deck, which the officers used to command and steer the ship. Lucy, next to him, smiled as he gave the orders to release the dock lines.

"Get yer head out of the clouds," Stinky bellowed, smacking the back of Christopher's head. "There's work to be done."

Stinky and the other man he had been talking to hoisted

the ramp that connected the boat to the wharf. With a weighty thud, the long heavy board landed on the deck.

Christopher second-guessed his decision to stay onboard as he watched lines being tossed from the shore to the ship. As soon as the lines were free, the men released the sails and the wind filled the creamy white canvas. The Captain called the orders while the men up on the yardarms trimmed the sails. The Georgiana inched away from the dock.

"Well, don't just stand there!" Stinky roared. "Get over here! This gangplank be need'n wash'n down and lash'n to the deck," he huffed, launching a bucket at Christopher's head. Christopher threw his hands up just in time to catch it.

The Georgiana sailed easily into the frothing brown water of the crowded bay. Christopher wondered about the destinations of the other ships. Theirs was not the fastest vessel in the harbor, but she was one of the biggest and the men onboard seemed excited about the adventure that lay ahead.

Christopher attached a line to the bucket and tossed it over the side of the ship to gather water. As he did, he noticed a smaller, faster schooner passing off the starboard side of the Georgiana. The name *Revenge* was painted on her transom.

Boots approached the rail. The menacing looking sailors onboard the schooner hooted. With a wave the

Revenge's captain, a man with an eye patch, pointed the sloop toward the mouth of the harbor.

"Set course," the Captain called to Mr. Johnson, the navigator, once they reached the open water. "It's time to head home."

"Aye, Captain," Mr. Johnson replied. "South by southwest it is."

CHAPTER 13

Christopher scrubbed every inch of the deck, then started coiling an unending supply of lines. Whenever Stinky walked past, he'd laugh and kick the newly formed coils, forcing Christopher to start over.

Christopher worked until he had blisters, and then until his blisters had blisters. At one point his hands started to bleed, but when he stopped to rub them Stinky hurled something at his head.

Lucy remained on deck all morning, walking past Christopher several times, but Christopher could do little but nod as Stinky never left his side.

When Stinky's watch was finally called below deck for their afternoon meal, an exhausted Christopher dropped his broom and followed the repulsive troll to the forward hatch.

"Where ye think ye be go'n boy?" he barked. Christopher looked confused. Ye not be hav'n no rest ye insolent barnacle scum! Ye may be finished scrub'n and coil'n but now ye get to polish."

His stomach rumbled in protest; Boots had eaten

Christopher's breakfast. Polish what? Christopher wondered until he heard the heavy clip clop of approaching boots.

Boots growled and passed Christopher a rag. "Them old guns there be need'n a good shine. If I don't see me own reflection in them when yer done, we'll see how well ye can swim."

"Mr. Jones," called one of the watch captains, the rugged, weathered old sailor Mr. Bruce, from above, "a minute please."

Boots turned to meet the man as he climbed down ratlines leading from the lookout perched high on the forward mast. Christopher fisted his hands and walked to a mounted swivel gun several yards down the deck.

"Blimey," Leo squeaked while scurrying up to Christopher at the rail. "I never thought those thugs would leave."

Christopher huffed as he started rubbing the gun. Leo scampered up his arm to sit in the crook of his neck as he continued to work. The messy gold curls that looped around Christopher's ears weren't quite long enough to be pulled back, but they were perfect for hiding a small mouse.

"Lesson Two," Leo squeaked. "Patience. It is, indeed, a virtue." His whiskers twitched. "Don't worry, Christopher. They'll ease up after a few days," he assured. Christopher sighed. "I may have to do something about your so-called uncle and his friend, however."

By dusk there was no sight of land or other ships from the deck of the Georgiana.

"Boy!" Boots called at last. "Come with me." Christopher tucked his rag into his tattered pants and set off in Boots' direction.

Chapter 14

The lamps were lit below decks. Laughter filled the ship after their day at sea. Someone was playing a fiddle in the distance. Christopher had not noticed the gentle rocking movement of the boat when he was up on deck during the day, but now with the lanterns lit and the smell of food coming from the galley, the sway was overwhelming him.

Cookie studied Christopher: ragged clothing, greenish skin, bags lining his eyes. An uncle should notice these things, but Mr. Jones seemed blind to them. Cookie had warned the Captain against hiring Mr. Jones, or as the crew called him, Boots. There was something about the look in his one good eye that Cookie did not trust, though all he had was a hunch and no proof. When their previous midshipman had failed to show after an evening ashore, the Captain was forced to make do with whomever was available. Cookie found it rather coincidental that Mr. Jones and his friend just happened to be on the dock waiting for an invitation. The whole situation had smelled fishy to him.

Cookie watched the boy. There was nothing in his interactions with Mr. Jones that would suggest any type of relationship. In fact, the child seemed scared of the man.

"Hmm," he grumbled, scratching his stubbled chin. "Supper?"

"Be gone with ye, Cookie. I've no time for ye now," Boots barked.

"Have it your way, Mr. Jones, but I've made a meal for both you and the boy."

Sugar ran to Christopher and climbed his leg so that she could wrap her long arms around his neck. "Eep!"

Christopher scratched her back.

Cookie had never had any children himself. He had wanted them, but things never quite worked out that way. Sure, there was Sugar, who meant as much to him as anyone ever could, but she was not a child. He looked over at Christopher again. I'll take care of you, lad, he vowed silently, pleased that Sugar had taken a liking to him. She was always a good judge of character.

"Put that monkey down!" Boots shouted.

Cookie smiled tightly while passing Christopher a plate with an extra portion of meat. Boots pulled Christopher away, forcing him to sit at the vacant table at the far side of the room.

"Top of the even'n" Stinky said, pushing in next to Christopher. He tore at his food with his hands while bits of gravy dribbled down his chin. Christopher pushed his bowl away.

Cookie approached with a bundle in his arms.

"What's this?" Boots growled as the old man set a blanket on the table. Next to the blanket lay stack of fresh clothing.

"These are for the boy. He will need them."

"He needs noth'n but me, old man."

"Captain's orders," said Cookie. He glanced at Christoper and added, "He will want to see the boy is being looked after."

"Ye saying I not be capable of minding the child?"

"Just carrying out the Captain's wishes."

"Then be off with ye. Ye done yer job."

"Very well." Again the old man looked at the boy. "Good night, Christopher."

"Good night yerself," Boots snarled.

When they reached the cabin after supper, Boots removed the keys from around his neck.

"Grab what we need," he ordered, tossing the keys to Stinky. With a *ca-chunk*, the lock gave way. Stinky lifted four carefully stowed bottles of rum from the trunk then reset the lock.

Boots looped the keys back around his bony neck and headed for the door with two bottles stowed under his arm.

"Best be get'n some sleep," Boots ordered. "Today was just a warm up."

Christopher lowered his weary body to the floor. Boots doused the lantern and the two men exited the room.

CHAPTER 15

As soon as the pirates disappeared, Leo slid under the door. "What a grumpy crab," he squeaked, relighting the lantern.

Christopher placed the bundle Cookie had given him on the bunk. There was a heavy woolen blanket; a clean, cream-colored, long-sleeved shirt; a pair of worn, tan short pants; a thick leather vest; and a small brown leather waist pouch.

Christopher stripped off the tattered remains of his old orphanage uniform, happy to be rid of it. The clean new clothes felt like heaven against his skin.

"Well, your smell has certainly improved!" Leo said, his whiskers twitching.

"Now, I have something for you, too."

Leo scurried off the table. He climbed the bull work that framed the door until he was even with the lock then jumped onto the door handle and inserted his tail into the lock.

"Be right back," he squealed as the door swung open.

Christopher peered down the abandoned hallway, an overwhelming sense of freedom filling his weary bones.

Within seconds Leo appeared dragging the same canvas food bag behind him that he had brought to Christopher in the storage hold.

"A gift from Sugar," he said with a smile. "She said you might be hungry."

"That is an understatement." Christopher's mouth watered.

"Sounds like that Stinky fellow is truly disgusting. According to Sugar, he even passed wind at the table."

Christopher gagged. "Ugh, don't remind me."

Christopher pulled out a chunk of soft fresh bread and a round of cheese that made Leo's eyes bulge.

"Want some?" Christopher asked, passing Leo a piece.

"Yes, please."

When Leo finished his cheese he stood. "I think from now on we should stick together."

"Okay," Christopher agreed.

"Pass me your pouch."

Christopher cocked his head to the side, handing Leo the leather satchel attached to the cord he tied up his short pants with.

With razor sharp teeth, Leo gnawed two small holes in the side of the bag. "So I can see," he said, looking up at Christopher. "And this," he continued, making several smaller incisions in the leather, "is for air circulation."

CHAPTER 16

Leo woke Christopher before the morning bells.

"What in tarnation?" Boots mumbled seeing the boy standing at the foot of his bunk. "If ye be up to trouble, I be feeding ye to the sharks," he warned.

Christopher bowed his head and shuffled after Boots as he left the cabin, Leo riding silently at his side.

"Good morning, Mr. Jones," Cookie said. Boots grabbed a warm biscuit from the bowl on the counter.

"And good morning, Christopher," Cookie said with a smile, seeing that the boy's new clothes fit perfectly. Christopher nodded and reached for a bun as Boots had done. He wouldn't make the mistake of going without breakfast again.

Fresh salty air filled Christopher's lungs as he stepped out upon the deck of the Georgiana. The wind had picked up a little since yesterday, and even though he could not see land, Christopher knew they were still close enough to have sea birds circling overhead.

"All right boy!" Boots snarled, turning to face Christopher as Stinky shoved him to his knees.

The corner of Stinky's lip curled. "Wet and sand the decks. I'll be back with a holly stone."

Sitting back on his heels, Christopher shook the hair from his face. He looked at the two buckets in front of him. One was filled with sand, the other with water. His brow raised as he wondered what he was supposed to do with them. The holly stone must be what he would use with the sand to scrub the dirt from the decks.

"Watch out!" Leo squeaked as a porous brick barreled toward Christopher's head.

"Get to work!" Stinky barked. Christopher stared at the stone on the deck. The pirate threw his hands into the air. "Pour the water, sprinkle the sand, then use yer holly to scrub it 'round," he growled, turning to leave.

"And don't let me catch ye lollygagging 'round or ye be meet'n the tip ah me boot," Stinky warned over his shoulder.

Leo fully emerged from his pouch and scampered up Christopher's arm to his shoulder. "That's it," he spat, straightening his cap, his whiskers quivering with anger.

Leo watched Stinky from across the deck, his black eyes shining in the morning sun. The man had a slight limp and could barely see his toes over the top of his belly. Sure, he had told Christopher that human guides no longer fought for their pupils, but he might have to break the rules in this case. He hated bullies. Leo's left ear twitched.

"I'll be back."

Leo darted down the deck, dashing between items so he wouldn't be seen. He was stronger than the average mouse as years of training helped him compensate for his size. With lightning speed he wove between Stinky's legs while grasping the end of a stray sail tie between his teeth. When he finished, he ran away squeaking.

Stinky's eyes bulged. "A mouse!" He licked his lips and gave chase, only to find himself flat on his back on the deck. The thick planks shuttered beneath his weight, and several crewmen standing close-by laughed, bruising not only the pirate's rump, but also his ego.

Three more times Stinky tried to get up but found himself on his backend. "Did you see him?" he yelled. "The devil who be doing this to me?"

Boots sneered. "What are you talking about, fool?"

"The wee mouse who be make'n me fall!"

"Get some rest," Boots warned as the watch bell chimed. "Ye'll be do'n no good if ye continue as ye are."

Chapter 17

"Hurry," Leo chanted. "If you finish your assigned work we can have a look around before Boots thinks to check in on you."

Christopher flashed Leo an excited grin while working faster than ever. Leo had been right; things were getting better with time. Christopher's hands were now used to the work and with Stinky humbled, the boy could breathe easier. When he finished, Christopher lifted Leo to his shoulder.

"Now," Leo whispered from behind a veil of Christopher's tresses. "Let's have a look around."

Leo led Christopher below deck where they peeked around doors into cabins Christopher had never noticed before. As they approached the mess, Leo tugged on Christopher's hair.

"Stop," he instructed. A lone sailmaker sat at one of the tables tending to a ripped sail. Leo pointed to two bulletins posted on the wall. "Read," he instructed. Christopher rolled his eyes. Leo raised his paw in the air. "Lesson One," he reminded.

*

Ship's Schedule

12:00 a.m.

-Second watch begins.

4:00 a.m.

-Third watch and idlers called.

6:00 a.m.

-Cook begins breakfast. Carpenters begin work.

7:00 a.m.

-Midshipman begins supervision.

7:30 a.m.

-Boatswain's mate uses the Boatswain's whistle and pipes. "All hands. Up hammocks."

8:00 a.m.

-Captain on deck.

-Mess tables lowered. Crew, lookout men, officers on duty, and second watch eat breakfast.

8:30 a.m.

-Third watch and remaining crew are called for breakfast. Gear stowed above deck. Lower decks cleaned and sponged down with vinegar.

-Watch begins to wet the decks. Sand sprinkled and decks scrubbed with holly stones. Broom and buckets used to clear the decks of sand and debris. Swabs used to dry the decks.

-Brass work shined.

9:00 a.m.

-Breakfast finished and regular duties begin.

11:00 a.m.

Captain:

-Views Midshipman's logs.

-Examines the boatswains, pursers, and carpenters accounts.

-Talks with Midshipman about who is on the blacklist.

-Calls all hands to witness punishment, if needed.

12:00 p.m.

-The navigator, navigator's mate, and midshipman use their sextants and quadrants to report that the sun has reached its meridian.

-Boatswain's mate pipes the crew, to dinner.

-Crew eats midday meal.

12:30 p.m.

-Midday meal is over.

-Grog is dispensed above deck. Fifer plays music.

1:30 p.m.

-Watch on deck is called to duty.

-Watch below deck sleeps or relaxes.

4:00 p.m.

-Crew is piped for supper. Second serving of grog.

5:00 p.m.

-All hands to quarters.

-Midshipman inspects men's quarters.

-Pumps rigged.

-Lifebuoys placed in position.

-Ship reported in good order to the Captain.

8:00 p.m.

-Hammocks are piped down.

-First watch begins.

*

As soon as Christopher finished, he moved on to the second bulletin. The man across the room from them whistled as he stitched.

*

<u>Rules</u>

No Theft

No Lying

No Swearing

No Mutiny

No Desertion

No Murder

No Sedition

No Blasphemy

No Firearms

All violators shall be dealt with swiftly and severely, according to the Captain's judgment!

*

The sailmaker stood, tucked the mended sail under his arm, and bid Christopher good day as he left to rejoin his mates on deck. Christopher nodded politely but waited until the man was gone until he spoke. Every day was organized with an efficiency that Christopher appreciated. The rules were straightforward and easy to understand. Following them to become an active member of the crew shouldn't be hard at all, Christopher thought.

"It's a shame most of the men onboard can't read," Leo said, as Christopher read through the rules a second time.

"Really?" Christopher whispered.

Leo nodded. "It's true. Most sailors can't read a thing."

Christopher could see a lantern burning in the galley.

"Let's go see what Cookie is doing," Leo said holding on to Christopher's ear.

When they rounded the corner into the galley, Christopher ran headfirst into Lucy. Her smile spread from one ear to the other, and for the first time since Boots told him of his plans Christopher wished he could speak.

"Hello," she piped. "We were just talking about you." Christopher's face turned red.

"My boy," Cookie greeted, waving a knife in the air before bringing it down to the board in front of him where he continued to chop onions. "Are you hungry? Can I get you something to eat?"

Christopher nodded, but before Cookie could hand him anything, Sugar screeched. Christopher's smile disappeared as he heard the heavy clop of boots.

"Quickly," the old man urged, motioning for the boy to duck below the counter.

"Have ye seen the boy?" Boots barked as he rounded the bend and met the old man's eyes.

Christopher held his breath.

Lucy cleared her throat. "Good afternoon, Mr. Jones."

"G'day, miss," Boots grumbled, reluctantly.

"Aye, I've seen him," Cookie stated calmly to Boots. "He was here a moment ago. I asked him if he might deliver something to the Captain for me. I hope you don't mind. He headed toward your cabin first; you might be able to catch him if you hurry."

"I do mind!" Boots yelled heading down the hall toward his cabin.

Cookie leaned back and eyed the crouching boy. "You best be off, son. I've only bought you a minute or two."

Christopher nodded.

"Be sure to be close to the Captain or one of the officers when your uncle comes 'round," Cookie warned. "He looked like he was about to blow a gale."

"Now wasn't that the most peculiar thing?" Lucy asked Cookie when they were alone in the galley again.

"That it was, Miss Lucy. I've been trying to put my finger on it since that boy first walked through my galley. Don't be telling your father I said so, but that there boy is no more related to that rogue than I am. He's got a good heart though, the boy—I can see that in his eyes. But what he's doing with the likes of Mr. Jones, I don't know."

"Cookie, you are always so suspicious," Lucy laughed. She loved her time down in the galley with the old man. He was like an uncle to her. Onboard, his job was to cook for the men, but behind closed doors he served as her father's truest friend and most trusted companion.

CHAPTER 18

Two nights later, Cookie approached the table at which Christopher and Boots sat eating supper.

"Mr. Jones," he said to Boots. "I was wondering if you would allow your nephew to help me out in the galley when he's finished working for you. I have asked the Captain if this arrangement would be acceptable, and he has agreed to it . . . if you do, of course."

Boots slurped the contents off his spoon. The day had not gone as he hoped, and he was feeling frustrated with the progress he and Stinky had been making with the crew of the Georgiana. Some of the men were refusing to turn.

Boots ran his hand over his mouth, wiping the grog from his lips.

"Why ye want the runt?" Boots asked.

"For serving and cooking," he replied. "I am undermanned and need an extra set of hands."

"Ye may have him then if you like, old man," Boots sneered. Christopher choked on the food he was chewing.

"Thank you, Mr. Jones," Cookie answered, smiling. "I'll be expecting you tomorrow afternoon then, Chris."

As the senior sailor left, Stinky leaned in. "What ye let'n go of the boy for, Boots?"

"Simple, ye fool. We need some time and a place to talk to the men. This gives us both." Then he turned to Christopher. "The stakes have risen now, crab bait. If ye make a mistake, I be kill'n the old man now too."

Christopher swallowed hard. He had wished for a job away from Boots, but now he regretted his thoughts because it was his fault Cookie's life was also in danger.

CHAPTER 19

"Here ye go, maggot," Stinky barked as he delivered Christopher to the galley the next afternoon. "If you utter a word, we'll kill you and that grisly old tuna, understand? I got eyes and ears all over the ship. Ain't noth'n go'n on I don't be know'n about!"

He was annoyed that Boots made him walk the boy down into the intoxicating hole when there'd be no food in it for him. It was one thing when there was a meal to be had, but when there was none, being here was just plain unfair. His stomach rumbled.

Christopher waited in the empty galley for Cookie to return. The room opened on one end with a tall counter spread across the gap for servicing the crew. A brick fire pit against the far wall held embers ready to be stirred to life when things needed to be cooked in the iron pot hanging from an arm fastened to the wall.

Christopher took a deep breath and was inhaling the rooms many scents when Sugar dashed toward him, chattering loudly.

"What is it, girl?" Christopher whispered, lifting her.

"Well hello there," Cookie said, emerging from the storage room he used as a pantry. He was covered in flour from head to toe. "Wasn't expecting you quite so soon but . . . " Cookie looked down at his shirt and dusted some flour from it.

"I'm glad you made it. Your timing seems to be spot on. I'm getting a bit too old for climbing."

The cook chuckled as he led Christopher into one of the two storage rooms he used for food. "You, on the other hand," he said, looking at Christopher, "are young, and by the looks of things, a good climber. Would you mind?" Cookie pointed up at a barrel.

Christopher smiled and retrieved the barrel.

"Now," Cookie said as he continued hauling the flour back into the main room. "I thought you could help me ready supper. After that I'll have you set up and serve the officers and Miss Lucy. They dine in the Captain's quarters." Cookie led Christopher over to a counter and passed him a knife from the drawer below.

"Lucy is about your age, Chris. Mind if I call you Chris? Thirteen if I'm right?"

Christopher nodded.

"Captain has three girls, all as pretty as can be, and another babe on the way, due any day actually. They live on a sugar plantation a few miles from the naval dockyard on the island of Antigua. One worked by all free hands. Have you ever been to Antigua, Chris?" Cookie eyed the boy looking for a reaction, but there was none.

"Aye, that'd be right. Your uncle said this is your first trip out at sea. Antigua, that'd be our homeport. The Captain says he's only got a few more crossings before he can retire and stay home with his wife and family. You see, this is why he'd be having the lovely Lucy with him. She's his youngest child until this next one is born. He's taken both of her older sisters on trips, so now it's Lucy's turn. He wants all his girls to see a bit of the world before he hangs up his sea bag. Personally, I think his heart breaks a little every time he leaves home, and having one of the girls with him eases the pain." Cookie heaved an enormous sack of potatoes on to the counter.

"Do you know how to peel a potato, Chris?" Christopher nodded again picking several from the sack. "Good, make sure to put them in here you're finished," he instructed, passing over a cast iron pot.

The hours passed so quickly that Christopher was shocked when Cookie asked him to lower the tables to set up for the evening meal. He felt for Leo in his pouch, forgetting that his mouse companion had taken off with Sugar shortly after he had arrived.

"I'll be having you go and set the Captain's table now,"

Cookie said. "Take the plates and the cutlery with you. The glasses, wine, and linens are there already."

CHAPTER 20

Christopher knocked on the Captain's ornately carved wooden door. When there was no answer, he turned the heavy brass lever. The portal opened, giving way to a large well-lit cabin at the back of the ship. Daylight poured in through the large aft windows that ran along the back wall of the cabin. In the center of the room was a large dining table with six sturdy chairs surrounding it. Bookshelves lined the starboard wall. An upright piano graced the far corner.

"Wow," Christopher breathed, amazed at the difference between this cabin and the others he had seen. He set his goods down on the buffet and walked over to the bookshelf. Christopher loved to read. Before his parents died, he had been his school's top student. He had even hoped to go to university some day. On one of the shelves next to a pile of books was a portrait of the Captain and his wife. She was holding a baby and two small children stood at their side. Christopher felt empty as he stared at the image.

A solid open desk sat near the back wall looking out over the water. Across it lay paper and a writing quill, along with several large drawings resembling maps.

On each side of the cabin were doors leading to bedrooms. He wondered which door lead to Lucy's. Tempted to look, he turned back to the work at hand.

Christopher laid Cookie's things out across the table. He scanned the cabinets for the other items he needed. He cleared the dining table and then laid a tablecloth across it. Cookie had given Christopher five sets of cutlery. As he set the table, he thought about who would be using the silverware. The Captain and Lucy, maybe the doctor and Mr. Johnson? He couldn't remember ever seeing either of them eating in the mess, but who was the fifth?

CHAPTER 21

Stepping back on the deck, Christopher noticed only a few crewmen in the rigging along with the Captain and Mr. Johnson at the helm. Cookie must have started serving supper. Christopher cursed himself for having taken so long. As he neared the forward hatch, Leo darted up his leg.

"How's it going?" the mouse panted, tickling Christopher's ear. The boy grinned.

"Where have you been all afternoon?" Christopher asked.

Lucy, walking up behind him, paused. "Excuse me?" Leo tucked behind Christopher's tangled hair. "Did you say something?" The color left Christopher's face. "I could have sworn you just asked where I had been?"

Christopher shook his head.

Lucy put her hands on her hips. "I know what I heard!"

Leo darted down the neck of Christopher's shirt and skittered out his pant leg. Christopher jumped at the feel of paws against his bare leg. Lucy shrieked as she saw the mouse scurry across the deck.

"What is that?"

Looking back up to Christopher for an answer, she found herself alone.

CHAPTER 22

"Humph." Lucy sank into the thick piles of blankets on her bunk.

"Eep," Sugar called out from the door.

"Hi, girl," Lucy said patting the bed beside her.

Sugar leapt onto the bunk.

"Christopher can talk," Lucy glowered, fisting her hands.

Sugar pulled Lucy's hair.

Lucy rubbed her head. "Ow! What was that for?"

"Ip, ip, ip," Sugar chattered.

Pushing Sugar aside, Lucy stomped across the small sleeping cabin to look out of the transom windows at the dark blue water. The weather was beginning to turn. She could see white caps starting to form on the tops of the swells.

Sugar stared up at her from on top of the pink quilt her mother had insisted she bring.

"Why did he lie to us?"

Sugar jumped down from the bed and walked toward the door.

"Where are you going?" Lucy harrumphed, picking her up. Sugar raised her leathery fingers to the girl's face. "Do you think I should tell Papa when he comes in?"

Sugar screeched and struggled to free herself from Lucy's grasp.

"Easy, girl," Lucy cooed, stroking Sugar's back. "I'll wait." Sugar nuzzled Lucy's neck. "I want to hear what he has to say for himself first."

CHAPTER 23

Christopher carefully balanced the trays of food for the Captain's table as he emerged from the fore cabin door. He looked for Lucy, but she was nowhere in sight. God only knows what she thought of him now.

"Mmm . . . ," Christopher murmured, breathing in the thick, salty air. Leo climbed onto his shoulder. "What do I do now?" he whispered to his companion.

"Wait," Leo told him. "Sugar went to see her. Lucy told Sugar she would talk to you before she did anything."

"Do you believe her?"

"I do."

Christopher counted to five while breathing deeply. "What do I tell Lucy when she asks?"

"Honesty is always the best policy." Leo grinned. "Lesson Three."

Christopher shook his head. "Now is not the best time for another lesson, Leo."

"I don't pick the timing, dear boy. Lessons simply present themselves when they are ready to be learned."

"Perfect." Christopher grimaced, adjusting the trays balancing in his arms.

"I think what you tell her is up to you," the little mouse squeaked. "But realize that she might not leave you alone until she knows the truth and that could put her in more danger than she is now."

Christopher closed his eyes. When he opened them, he saw sailors climbing the aft ratlines. The familiar moan of yardarms filled the air as the sails were trimmed taking on new positions.

A strong puff of wind caught Christopher's hair, wiping it against his cheeks. "Did you feel that?"

"Yes," Leo licked his finger and raised it above his ears to the breeze. "It's coming from the north. I hope we're not in for a storm."

Dark clouds crowded the horizon.

"Better get going," Leo warned.

CHAPTER 24

"Good evening," the Captain greeted. "Come in." The warm light of the bright cabin engulfed Christopher.

The men huddled around the chart table looked up. Lucy, who had been reading in an overstuffed chair in the corner of the room, placed her book to the side and watched as Christopher set a heavy silver soup bowl on the table. Christopher could feel her eyes on him. The hairs on the back of his neck stood on end.

"Here," said a man Christopher recognized from up on the aft poop deck. With a finger on the chart on the table, the man continued. "This is where we shall enter the islands. Road Town is less than a day's sail once we pass through Anagada Channel. It is the widest of the channels, and we are less likely to be spotted if we sail right down the center."

Christopher had not formally met the man yet, but he had been studying him. He did not mingle with the rest of the crew and had an air of authority about him that invited little conversation.

"Thank you, Christopher," the Captain said, turning away from the desk of men. "Have you met everyone?" It was not uncommon for men of all ranks on a merchant vessel to socialize while out at sea. Christopher shook his head.

"Well then," he started, "you know my daughter, Lucy." Christopher bobbed his head.

"And this is the ship's doctor, Mr. Miller." Christopher's hand disappeared in the doctor's larger one. Metal half-glasses perched on the end of his nose.

The Captain continued. "This is Mr. Johnson, our chief navigator."

"I have seen you up on deck. You are a hard worker," Mr. Johnson said while extending his hand, which made Christopher smile. Mr. Johnson's deeply lined eyes spoke of years in the sun.

The man at the back of the room standing by the aft hull lights cleared his throat. He made no move forward and kept his arms pinned behind his back. His stony gaze swept the boy's body, sending a shiver down his spine.

"Yes, where are my manners?" The Captain's voice sounded strained and his posture became rigid. "Christopher, this is Admiral Cunningham of Her Majesty's Royal Navy. He is our guest for this passage."

The Admiral snorted.

"Shall we sit?" the Captain asked, gesturing to the steaming food placed on the table. "We can continue our conversation there as long as Lucy doesn't mind."

"Papa," Lucy said with a shake of her head, "since when have I had a say in what is discussed at the table?"

Admiral Cunningham turned toward Christopher and looked him over. "Is the boy safe?"

"Cookie would not have sent him to us if he had any doubts. In addition, Christopher cannot speak, so our security is assured."

Lucy's chocolate gaze locked on Christopher's as the boy moved to the water pitcher. His hands shook as he filled the men's cups.

The cutlery clicked against the fine china as the guests started to eat. Christopher stepped away from the table, busying himself with the remaining platters of food at the buffet.

Mr. Johnson tapped his plate with his knife to get everyone's attention. "Admiral Cunningham, the islands to the north are more secured. You have to remember we are a merchant vessel, not a warship. Escape is virtually impossible if we run into trouble."

"Yes. Do not think I haven't weighed this issue over in my mind. Our mission, however, is to deliver the cargo as quickly as possible."

Mr. Johnson inhaled and placed his soiled napkin on the table. "If you choose to sail through the Anagada Channel, Captain, then we must alter our course."

The Captain ground his teeth. "Do as the Admiral wishes, Mr. Johnson."

The Captain knew these waters far better than the Admiral, and he did not like having another man call the shots on his ship. In fact, he did not like anything about his new cargo or the esteemed Admiral Cunningham. The sooner he could get both off of his ship, the better.

CHAPTER 25

As the officers dined, Christopher wandered over to the bookcase against the far wall of the cabin. He recognized a couple of the titles such as *Robinson Crusoe* and *Gulliver's Travels*, but most of the other books were new to him. Christopher fingered the gold lettering on the spine of *Robinson Crusoe*. He remembered his father reading it to him in front of the fireplace at home. It had been his favorite.

The Georgiana rocked from side to side, tossed between the increasing waves. The rolling motion of the sturdy ship seemed to alarm only him, making it harder to concentrate. Christopher stumbled as the Georgiana lurched forward, forcing him to grab the wall rail to steady himself.

Lucy glanced up from her conversation with Mr. Miller and noticed Christopher looking at her father's books. How odd, she thought. Why would he be looking at their books, unless . . . he reads? She knew he could speak; that she was sure of. The fact that he could read and might have had some sort of education most certainly meant that he could not have come from the same family as that awful man, Mr. Jones. An idea stirred in her head.

"Christopher," the Captain beckoned. The boy turned his attention to the table, leaving his gloomy thoughts with the golden titles he had just read. "The weather is picking up. I believe it is time to clear and tie things down. Please take the remains of our supper back down to Cookie with our compliments."

The Captain and his men reached for their coats and headed out on deck. When the door opened, Christopher noted that the seas had indeed gotten bigger. As the Georgiana hit each oncoming wave, the ship was doused in saltwater making the decks slippery and hard to maneuver. As he struggled against the wind to close the cabin door, the Captain shouted orders to take in the fore and aft mizzenmast sails.

"Lucy, my love," the Captain said, turning back to his daughter, "secure the cabin."

"Yes, Papa," she answered. She had sailed through two other storms such as this on their first trip across the Atlantic. She knew what to do.

Christopher quickly gathered the dishes. Lucy put little things such as table lamps, books, and pictures into heavy sea chests.

"Wait!" Lucy called to Christopher when he was nearly out the door. "This is for you," she said, handing him a book. "Just make sure to bring it back when you're finished." Christopher glanced at the title. It was the copy of *Robinson Crusoe* he had been looking at, but he noticed a note was tucked inside the cover. "Now if you'll excuse me, I need to stow the things in my father's cabin."

Christopher opened the book and read the piece of paper lying between the pages.

We need to talk. I'll find you in the morning when your uncle is below decks.

-L

Christopher opened one of the heavy sea chests and lay the book inside hoping Lucy would understand why he could not take it. He did not leave the note, however. That he ripped into tiny shreds to burn in the galley's brick oven.

Clutching the last of the plates, he braced himself against the wall, arms full, and attempted to open the door. A slap of seawater greeted him. The salt stung his eyes, and his throat burned as he coughed up the uninvited liquid. After securing the door behind him, he stumbled across the deck.

"What the . . . who the . . . ," Christopher heard Leo hail from inside his pouch. "Now that's no way to wake up! Christopher what's going on?" Leo popped his head out, mopping the wet tuft of fur from his eyes.

Lines dangled from the yardarms as the Captain called the men aloft to take in the topgallant sails. The wind howled through the rigging. The grey sky now matched the color of the churning sea. Mr. Johnson wrestled control of the wheel as the Captain assessed the situation on deck and made sure all safety precautions were being met.

"'Tis a heck of a blow, Captain, but we have seen far worse. I am afraid we are in for a long night!" Mr. Johnson yelled over the storm.

"Tighten the shrouds and batten down all the hatches, men, for we don't want to be manning the pumps before morning," the Captain ordered.

The soft creaking sounds the ship normally made in flat water were replaced by the crashing sounds of items improperly stowed. Christopher couldn't tell whether he should duck or jump as he made his way through the chaos.

When he finally reached the galley, he stored the few items that remained in his hands and made his way to the old brick oven. As he tossed the torn scraps of Lucy's note inside, he realized that the slowly burning embers that were usually there, ready for whatever needed to be cooked, had been doused. The only thing left burning in the galley at the moment was the wildly rocking lantern hanging from the ceiling.

Christopher looked at the pieces of paper. Fire or not, they'd be gone soon enough, he thought.

Christopher took Leo from his pouch and placed him safely on the counter. "I'm going to go find Sugar," he squeaked, wringing out his hat.

"Christopher!" Cookie yelled from across the room. "If we don't get these water barrels properly tied down we are all in trouble."

The violent movement of the ship turned Christopher's stomach.

"All hands!" came the call from above.

"Right we go, Chris! She'll be bucking like a newborn stallion up on deck. Don't you worry though! I got eyes in the back of my head and one will be on you. I'll be right behind you as soon as I go check on Lucy." The Georgiana groaned, complaining loudly as she struggled against the storm.

"Sugar!" Cookie yelled. The monkey appeared out of nowhere and stood at attention in the middle of the narrow hallway. "The galley is yours, girl. You know what to do. Keep clear. I'll be back for you soon enough."

Cookie paused at the end of the counter. "Remember, Chris, it's a different game on deck when the winds blow like this. At times it will seem as though you can touch Neptune himself. If they send you up in the rigging, look up and forward. Never look down. Concentrate on your feet and where you put your hands. The higher up you climb, the more you'll swing."

Christopher felt Leo scurry up his pant leg. "Put me on your shoulder. There's no time to lose," Leo ordered, grabbing a handful of Christopher's curls. "Let's go!"

Chapter 27

Bam!

An explosion rocked the ship just as Christopher and Leo entered the gun deck on their way to the Captain. Ropes once tied to the floor flew through the air and fragments of splintered wood littered their path.

"Run!" Leo squeaked, realizing what had happened just in time to see one of the far port side main guns come barreling toward them.

"What's going on?" Christopher panted, leaping out of the way as the enormous iron beast crashed into the side of the hull.

"She's broke her fittings," Leo squeaked.

Sure enough, each time the Georgiana bucked from wave to wave, the demonic gun spun, destroying everything in its path.

Christopher gawked at the debris, feeling certain that the hull would be pierced if they did not act soon.

Water gushed through the grating above as the ship hit yet another wave. Christopher scanned the room.

"The cargo net!" he cried, darting through the ruin.

The Georgiana ricocheted off a wave and started to heel in the opposite direction.

"We have to stop it or it will sink the ship!" Leo yelled. Christopher tied two corners of the net to a support beam while Leo grabbed the opposite edge between his teeth and hurried to the iron eye used to secure barrels to the inner deck.

"Can you get something to wedge behind the wheel when it hits the net?" Christopher asked, realizing that stopping the gun would not be enough. They would have to tie it down if they were to save the Georgiana.

The shipboard cannon started toward the net.

"What's going on in here?" Admiral Cunningham asked, stepping through the open doorway, the sound of the storm raging around them, swallowing his voice. Christopher's eyes darted between the Admiral and the gun. "Your Captain ordered all hands on deck! I'll see you whipped for your insolence!"

With the force of a charging bull, the big gun smashed into the Admiral's side launching him across the room and then continued toward the net at full speed. The Admiral landed on the planking opposite them and did not move.

As the gun struck the makeshift barricade, the two friends heard the knots tighten and stretch.

The net absorbed the gun's force allowing Leo to grab

a barrel fragment to shove beneath the rear wheel. The big gun bucked, breaking free. Christopher dove as the iron beast spun, shoving a second wooden brace in place.

The cabin stilled, the gun frozen in place.

CHAPTER 28

Water poured down on them from the grate above. Christopher grabbed one of the lines still hanging from the rafters securing the gun to the deck.

"Over here!" Leo cried from atop the Admiral's motionless body. "He's still breathing."

Christopher carefully turned over the unconscious Admiral. Blood oozed from a deep gash in his upper leg.

"Rip off his pant leg where it has been torn and roll it into a bandage so we can stop the bleeding!" Leo ordered.

The Georgiana heeled to the side. Christopher could barely see through the waterlogged wreckage and now he had the Admiral's leg and maybe life to save. He gasped, trying to regain control. His mind spun.

"All hands!" Christopher heard the Captain call again.

The mouse pressed the fabric roll into the wound. "Find Mr. Miller."

Christopher ran out on to the main deck. Men clung to the yardarms and yelled hopelessly against the howling wind. The Georgiana barreled into mountain after mountain of frothing grey surf. A wave crashed over the rail nearly taking Christopher with it. Mr. Miller stood next to the Captain on the poop deck.

Clinging to the rail, Christopher made his way toward the officers. One step. Another step. The gale force winds pushed against him making it difficult to advance. He looked down to the main deck to see Boots charging toward him. Reaching the officers, Christopher grabbed Mr. Miller's arm.

"What is it, boy?" Mr. Miller yelled angrily. "Can't you see we're busy?"

Christopher shook his head and tried to pull the doctor toward the main cabin.

"Sorry, sir, I don't know what he be think'n," Boots growled. He latched onto Christopher's shoulders shaking the boy roughly, but Christopher refused to release the doctor.

"For God's sake, follow the boy!" the Captain ordered, seeing the commotion. "Can't you see he needs you?"

"Mercy be," Mr. Miller hissed, as they entered the demolished gunroom. The Admiral lay in a heap on the floor. Mr. Miller gasped. "Christopher, is this what you were trying to tell us?"

"Christopher!" Cookie panted, running into the room. "Thanks be to God, you're safe! You had me worried." He had seen Christopher out of the corner of his eye, then watched as Boots and Mr. Miller followed him below decks.

"Yes, Cookie, but the Admiral is not," Mr. Miller said, shaking his head. "He's lost a lot of blood. Help me get him to the infirmary. We have to stabilize him if he's to have a fighting chance."

Cookie nodded.

"And you two best be getting back up on deck," he said to Boots and Christopher.

CHAPTER 29

Boots gripped Christopher's arm tightly, nearly tearing it from the socket as they crossed the fore hatch and stepped onto the deck.

"Arrgh boy, ye done good. That admiral be a pain in me backside. With him in the infirmary, me job gets a wee bit easier." A long, crooked sneer spread across the pirate's jagged face.

A lightning bolt lit the sky, thunder exploded, and the boat shuddered.

"Christopher!" the Captain shouted. "Take Mr. Cullen's place in the rigging."

Christopher looked up. His body shook.

Mr. Cullen, a hardened sailor, clutched his bloodied arm to his chest.

"Find Mr. Miller, and have that arm looked at immediately," the Captain ordered.

Christopher approached the rail. The Georgiana pitched violently to starboard as another wave broke across her bow.

Christopher had twice climbed the rope ladders that

led to the platforms the sailors used to adjust the sails and look upon the horizon but both times were in calm seas. The first time, when Mr. Bruce, the watch captain, had shown him how, had been exciting. He loved the way the sky stretched forever from atop the mast. He wanted to spend more time aloft but then Boots had called him down, forcing him to leave. The second time Stinky had ordered him to do what he was too lazy to do himself.

Another bolt of lighting flashed its spiny fork coming within a boat's length of the Georgiana.

"Up the foremast you go," Boots barked. "Out the yardarm and secure the sail. I've got five quid resting on ye not making it through the night."

Christopher grabbed the ratline and swung his feet onto the guardrail. He thought about what Cookie had said. Eyes straight, watch your footing, concentrate, never look down.

"Up, boy, and I mean now!" Boots yelled.

Out of the corner of his eye, Christopher spotted Leo's red cap darting toward him. As a wave slapped Christopher in the face, the ship rolled back to port. Hand over hand, he started climbing.

"Wait for me!" Leo panted, catching Christopher. The ship swayed violently to starboard.

Christopher turned white as a freshly laundered sheet and his grip tightened upon the line.

"The only thing to fear is fear itself!" Leo yelled from the rung next to his ear. Christopher paused for a moment and looked at Leo. "Lesson Four," the mouse said with a twitch of his whiskers. He then clutched onto the back of Christopher's shirt and whispered, "Shut out the storm."

As Christopher reached the first fore topmast platform, the sail ripped from the sailor's grip, breaking the yardarm in half.

Lightning flashed and thunder cracked.

Fragmented lines and halyards whipped wildly against wet canvas. In the remains of the tangled rigging, two of the seven men that had been on the arm hung by their legs. The remaining sailors scampered to the uppermost platform and pulled one of the two men to safety.

Christopher wrapped his arms around the mast and watched as the remaining crewman's eyes rolled back in his head. The ship hurled forward. The unconscious man swung toward the platform.

"Hurry!" shouted Henry, one of the sailors, from above. "She's coming down!"

Without thinking, Christopher reached for the crewman.

"Grab on!" Leo squeaked from his shoulder.

"The sail's breaking apart!" a crewman yelled.

Christopher braced his weight against the lines attached to the mast and gripped the sailor's shirt. Mr.

Bruce hurried down the ratlines and pulled Christopher and the injured sailor back on to the topmast platform. Mr. Bruce pulled a rigging knife from his boot and frantically cut away at the tangled web connecting his friend to the failed rigging, freeing him.

"She's coming down!" cried a sailor.

Another wave hit and tossed the Georgiana back to port. The shredded sail and smaller half of the severed yardarm tumbled toward the deck. The ship rebounded to starboard as another wave crashed over her bow. The yardarm plunged into the sea. The men on the deck gathered at the rail trying to salvage what they could.

Christopher stared in disbelief as the sailors jumped to their feet. What remained of the larger half of the battered yardarm was coming toward them. Mr. Bruce grabbed the wounded sailor and rushed him down the ratlines to Mr. Miller. The remaining men braced for impact. With a crash, the yardarm hit the topmast.

"Grab here and pull!" the men surrounding him hollered.

Christopher struggled against the weight of the water-soaked canvas, pulling on the sail, while more sailors lashed down what they could of its tattered remains.

Hours passed as Christopher worked side by side with the other sailors on the platform. Just as the winds were weakening, the sail and yardarm were finally secured.

Christopher looked to the east and noticed the slightest shimmer of orange lighting the horizon.

"The sun's coming up," Leo whispered from behind a mass of tangles.

Mr. Bruce approached. "Go down and get yourself some rest, pup. You done good."

CHAPTER 30

Christopher collapsed on the floor in his cabin's corner. He was exhausted, but still he couldn't sleep. Flashbacks from the night before invaded his thoughts. Every sound he heard made him think the wind had picked up again.

Just as he started to doze off, Boots crashed into the stateroom. "Boy!" he yelled, kicking Christopher. "Ye cost me money tonight."

Christopher glared at Boots. He hated him. It took everything he could muster not to fight back, to have patience, to remain silent.

"Get out!" Boots spat. "I need me beauty rest."

Christopher hurried out of the cabin before he lost his temper and stumbled sleepily through the empty galley.

"I'm going to go find Sugar," Leo said, peeking out of the pouch and scratching his salt-crusted fur.

Remnants of the damage inflicted by the storm littered the cabins he passed. The gun deck was in ruins. Blood still stained the floor where the Admiral had collapsed.

When he finally reached the main deck, the clouds had disappeared and the sun was just starting to dry out the waterlogged deck. The Georgiana gently hummed as she cut through the untroubled seas. The noise was soft and reassuring, nothing like the night before. Everything seemed relatively peaceful. Christopher took a deep, relaxing breath of the heavy sea air. The wind had clocked around, now coming from behind. It felt as though the Georgiana was being guided through the water instead of fighting against it as it had done during the storm. It was amazing what the sea was capable of. He would never doubt its strength again.

The Captain must have decided to give the sailors a break, he thought, for he had not heard the watch bell ring in hours. Mr. Johnson was at the helm and only a skeleton crew remained on deck. Christopher looked for Cookie, but he was nowhere in sight.

With no one pressing him to work, he walked over to the guardrail and stared out over the endless water. Small fish played in the waves beside the boat. They glided across the water, staying above the surface for minutes at a time. Their silver bodies glittered in the sunlight, and their fins looked like wings. Christopher stared, mesmerized. He had never seen anything like them before. Were they even fish or were they some sort of curious sea bird? So preoccupied by these strange new creatures, Christopher failed to hear the footsteps approaching him from behind.

"They are called flying fish," Lucy said, standing next to him.

Christopher's heart stopped. He scanned the deck making sure they were alone.

"Yes," he said quietly.

The sound of his voice sent a shiver down Lucy's spine. "Why did you lie about being able to talk?"

"I didn't have a choice."

Lucy tilted her head to the side. "What do you mean?"

Christopher took a deep breath. "Lucy, the man who claims he's my uncle is no relation to me. If I don't do what he says, he will kill me. Now that I am working with Cookie he said he would kill him too. And if he sees us together, you will be next on his list." Christopher sighed and his head sank in defeat.

Lucy's eyes grew large. "Why? I don't understand?"

"He and his friend Stinky are pirates. They are after the guns the Georgiana is carrying."

"But we don't carry guns . . . just mail, silks, cargo that is no value to pirates." Lucy crossed her arms. "You must be mistaken."

"I wish I was."

Lucy shook her head. She could not believe what Christopher was saying.

"It is true, Lucy. I am sorry to be the one to tell you."

Lucy thought about Christopher's words for a few

seconds. "Then we have to tell my father. He can put a stop to this."

"No," Christopher said flatly.

"What do you mean? Of course he can stop this. He is the Captain."

"He won't believe me, Lucy. It would be my word against Boots', and I'm just a kid who has already been lying to him this whole time. I need proof if I am going to accuse one of his junior officers." Christopher looked down at the deck. "And I don't have any."

The words she wanted to stay stuck in her throat. He was right.

"I have to do this on my own," he said. "I don't want to be responsible for something happening to you, too. As soon as I find something, I will let you know. Until then, you need to stay away from me."

"No!"

"It's too dangerous, Lucy."

"I'll figure something out," she said, already thinking about what kind of proof they would need to go to her father.

"Lucy, stay out of it! I mean it!" The watch bell rung for the first time that morning and Christopher tensed. "I need to go."

Stinky and the rest of his watch emerged from the forecastle, and Christopher walked toward them leaving Lucy standing at the rail.

"Eep!" Sugar called, bounding down the rail toward Lucy.

Lucy's nose wrinkled as she noticed a passenger upon the monkey's back. Sugar stopped in front of her and Leo slid to his feet. He smoothed his ears and said, "Mademoiselle," as he bowed deeply.

Lucy gasped.

"Chi chi chi," Sugar chattered.

"Until next time!" Leo said and scurried away.

Lucy's chin dropped.

Chapter 31

Cookie was already prepping the afternoon meal when Christopher reached the galley.

"Glad to see you out and about, lad," he greeted.

The few men still lingering about in the mess and sipping their last dregs of watered-down coffee looked up.

"You're quite the hero, Chris," Cookie said. "First you save the Admiral, then Big John. You might have even single-handedly saved the entire ship when you lashed down that big gun." Cookie patted Christopher on the back. "I haven't figured out how you handled that beast by yourself, but I'm mighty glad you did! The Captain is darn right happy with you, too."

Leo's fourth lesson repeated in Christopher's head. He had been terrified when he climbed the ratlines during the storm, but he did not hesitate to reach for Big John, which would have been much scarier had he thought about it at the time. Maybe the mouse was right? Fear only exists in your head. Christopher smiled. Embarrassed, he turned and grabbed the stained apron hanging from the hook. He tied it loosely around his waist and started to tidy up the galley.

The oven fire was burning brightly. Christopher smiled again as he could not see the remnants of the Lucy's note. He was glad it had been destroyed.

"The Admiral's leg is mangled, but he'll make it, thanks to you. Big John, the man you pulled from the rigging, has a few cuts and a bump the size of a sounding ball on his head, but after a little rest and some of my stew he should be good as new, too. He's back in his hammock now with Mr. Bruce watching over him." Cookie wiped his hands on his apron. "Think I'll have you deliver some biscuits and grog to the forecastle around midday so you can check on him yourself."

CHAPTER 32

The heavy wooden door to the crew's quarters creaked as Christopher pushed it open. The forecastle was a common room where the sailors slept in the front of the boat, not far from the main deck. It was also where Boots did most of his recruiting.

The rancid odor of dirty men wafted through the room making Christopher gag. A lantern burned in the back of the chamber, and a half dozen men hunched around a makeshift barrel table. Christopher carefully picked his way through the maze of hammocks, which hung from the ceiling in every direction and were heavily weighed down by bodies. Rotting wooden sea chests littered the floor.

Every sailor onboard was given a sea chest when he was assigned to a hammock, and it was his only private space on the ship. In these roughly constructed two by three foot boxes, a seaman had to stow all of his belongings.

The man at the table closest to Christopher turned. Sweat trickled down his temples and glistened in the light of the lantern's flame.

"What are ye do'n here?" Stinky growled from the stool next him. He stood. "I asked ye a question, ye rat scum!" Stinky yelled as he approached.

Seeing nothing but rage in the ogre's bloodshot eyes, Christopher held the biscuits out in front of him.

"Be still," a commanding voice bellowed from one of the hammocks. "He's only brung us food and drink from the galley."

"Aye, 't-tis true," the sweating man shuddered.

Christopher left the food on the table. Backing away, he tripped over an open trunk.

The men around Stinky stood.

Embarrassed and awash with fear, Christopher struggled to stand. Dirt-crusted clothing, a folded letter, and a pistol spilled out of the trunk and onto the floor.

"Ye bloody fool!" Stinky cussed.

"Here," the voice who had championed Christopher offered. "Take my hand."

Mr. Bruce pulled Christopher to his feet.

"There's no good reason for you to be in here," Mr. Bruce warned, escorting Christopher to the door. "Next time, knock and leave your goods there." He pointed to a barrel just inside the door before opening the door and ushering Christopher out.

CHAPTER 33

The sails on the Georgiana lay limp and still over the yardarms like the laundry Christopher's mother used to hang out to dry on hot, windless summer days. Since the storm two days ago, not even the slightest breath of wind had crossed the deck. The ocean resembled a looking glass.

The heat of the afternoon left Christopher longing to jump into the welcoming blue water to cool off, but he had been warned by stories of those who had succumbed to the temptation of diving in only to be eaten by the sharks that lay waiting in the cool shadows of the ship or left to drown when they were unable to climb back onboard. Christopher contented himself with dumping the occasional bucket of seawater on his head while scrubbing the decks.

He still had no proof to convict Boots and his friend, but he knew that the crew had guns and that the Captain did not allow his men to carry weapons onboard his ship. It wasn't sufficient, yet it was something—maybe enough to earn some credibility if he told the Captain and he called for a search. Still the pistol could be long gone by now. Then Christopher would look more the fool than before.

On the third sizzling day, Lucy waited for him in the galley. He heard her voice before he could see her. Leo scampered down the back of Christopher's untucked shirt and ran off to find Sugar before he rounded the corner.

"Hi, Christopher," Lucy beamed. Cookie chopped onions on the countertop next to her.

Christopher eyed her suspiciously. She smiled sweetly, batting her lashes. Christopher's inner warning alarm went off. She had not listened to him.

"I brought you this," Lucy said, presenting Christopher with a few books. Christopher glared at her.

"I didn't know you could read," Cookie said, looking up from his onions.

"Oh, it's just a guess, Cookie. I keep catching him looking at our bookshelf," Lucy said.

"Is it true then, Chris?" Cookie asked. "Can you read?"

Christopher nodded.

"Well I'll be, Lucy love, you have the eyes of an angel. Thank goodness someone noticed. Does this mean you've had some learning then?" Cookie asked eagerly, watching Christopher closely for a response. When he saw what he needed, a nod from Christopher, he clapped his hands together in joy. "Do you know what this means, son?"

Christopher shrugged.

"No more menial tasks for you. There's more in your future than just swabbing the decks. Does your uncle know?"

Horror flooded Christopher's face. He had a pretty good idea that Boots wouldn't be happy about Cookie's discovery.

Christopher pushed the books back toward Lucy, shaking his head.

"I think he is worried about his uncle not wanting him to have the books," Lucy told Cookie a little too cheerfully. Christopher narrowed his eyes toward her as steam poured from his ears.

"It's okay, Chris. You pass them books to me. I'll take care of your uncle," Cookie said with a wink.

Christopher pressed his palm to his throbbing head and left.

CHAPTER 34

Cookie gathered up several books into a pile and approached Boots' table.

"These," he said loudly, "are for the boy." Christopher cringed at the pirate's side. "I'll be having him manage the supper tomorrow," Cookie said to Boots, and then, turning to Christopher added, "and these here are the recipes you'll be needing, lad."

Boots grabbed the book on the top of the stack and inspected it.

"Are you a reader, Mr. Jones?" Cookie asked innocently, already knowing the answer. Boots looked at him with his steely grey eyes and tossed the recipe book to the table.

"I got no time for such matters and neither does the boy. I don't want them things clutter'n up me cabin, old man."

"Well that's just too bad," Cookie insisted. "Unless you'd like me to take up the issue with the Captain? If he's going to work with me, he'll be needing to read these."

Boots grunted, stood, and pounded his fist on the table. "Watch yer tone with me, old man!"

Cookie's brow raised as Boots stormed off toward his cabin.

"Don't you worry, " Cookie whispered to Christopher. "I'll still be making supper. I just wanted you to have a chance to take something to your cabin to read. These are recipes, stories, and botany books for you to have a look at."

"Boy!" Boots howled, his voice echoing down the dimly lit corridor.

Christopher nodded to Cookie and ran after Boots clutching the pile of books to his chest.

CHAPTER 35

"But Captain, he's just a mute," Boots repeated when the Captain said he would like to have Christopher join Lucy for lessons during their morning meeting. "I don't know what me sister was think'n teach'n him to read. His future be with me."

"Mr. Jones, don't you think we should give the boy a chance? Do you not want him to better himself? Becoming something more?"

"No! The boy's my responsibility. He don't need to be learn'n anythin' more than what I be teach'n him. His life be mine and I'll be do'n what I please with it."

The Captain looked upon Mr. Jones's face, surprised by his candor. Did he not remember with whom he was talking?

"Now, Mr. Jones," the Captain said more forcibly, "I do not know what the agreement is between you and your sister, but I am insisting that you allow the boy a chance at an education so long as he's on my ship."

Boots sneered and his brow creased.

"I will expect him at my cabin as soon as he is done

with his morning chores so that he can join Lucy in her lessons. Do you understand?"

"Aye, sir. I do," Boots growled.

Chapter 36

"Boy!" Boots hollered as he stomped into the cabin after his meeting. He stooped down, grabbed Christopher by the front of his shirt, and pinned him to the cabin wall.

"Ye and them damn books!" he spat, spying a book on the ground.

Leo twitched beneath the spine of the text they had been reading on indigenous plants of the Caribbean.

The door flew open, startling Boots, and he dropped Christopher to the floor.

"What's going on?" Stinky asked breathlessly. "I saw ye rush'n down this direction and heard ye yell'n. Do we get to kill the bilge rat now?" Stinky pointed a crooked finger in Christopher's direction and licked his crusty lips.

"No, ye dolt. Seems our boy here is destined for bigger things. Captain's got it in his head that he should be educated; insists on it. Says Miss Lucy be hav'n lessons, and the boy is to join her. Damn that stupid girl! She'll get hers soon enough!" Boots snarled.

Stinky scratched his chest, frowning. "We should feed him to the sharks. I could make it look like an accident."

Christopher's eyes bulged. Boots began to pace the room. "It be too late for that now."

Stinky shook his head. His fingers caressed the hilt of the dagger tucked in his sash. "Damn."

Boots placed his shiny black boot on Christopher's chest pinning him to the ground. "Remember," he said bringing his index finger against his throat, his Adam's apple bobbing as he dragged his finger across it. "Do anythin' to give us away and there be a fate worse than death for ye." Boots lifted his foot and Christopher squirmed to the side.

Stinky snorted. "We be the ones in charge of this ship now, boy. Don't ye forget it."

CHAPTER 37

A gentle breeze caught the sails and slowly pushed the Georgiana through the crystal blue water. It was the first sign of wind in almost a week, and it seemed to put everyone onboard in a good mood. Christopher quickly finished his work on deck and then headed to the galley to see what Cookie needed before reporting to the Captain's cabin for his first lesson.

"Christopher," Mr. Bruce bellowed from aloft, "come up here with me, boy."

Christopher climbed the ratlines. When he reached the platform Mr. Bruce offered him a hand. "Welcome aloft."

The watch captain was not a tall man per se, but thick and sturdy and easily the strongest man on the ship.

"I've got something to show you." He passed Christopher his spyglass. The worn leather and brass casing warmed his hand. He had seen spyglasses before but had never held one.

"See there," Mr. Bruce instructed and pointed ahead. "In the distance."

Christopher stretched the looking glass out and held it

to his eye. It took him a while to find what Mr. Bruce was pointing at. "Them be the first signs of land."

Christopher choked.

A group of white birds circled close to the water's surface on the horizon. "Them birds be fish'n now, but they be land dwellers when they're not hunting." Christopher lowered the spyglass to his side, regarding the weathered sea dog.

"Christopher," Mr. Bruce said squinting into the sun before looking at him in the eyes, "you seem like a nice lad, but those men you be hanging around with are up to no good. Family or not, as soon as we hit land, I want you to run. Run as fast and as far as you can. Don't stop for noth'n. I've seen you work. I know you've got heart. You put it all on the line when you saved Big John, and he and I have been mates for a long time. It was my watch he was on when he got hurt, so I figure we both owe you." He placed his meaty hand on Christopher's shoulder. "Being on the water for as long as we have can make men, even good men, do things they know they ought not to."

Christopher nodded, though he wasn't sure what Mr. Bruce was talking about.

Mr. Bruce took several deep breaths and stared out over the endless blue water. "It shouldn't be much more than a couple of days till we see land. If we're lucky we'll make port the night after that."

CHAPTER 38

"Afternoon, Christopher," the Captain welcomed as he opened the cabin door. "Cookie told me you can read. Can you write as well?"

Christopher nodded.

The chart table had been cleared. A writing quill and several pieces of blank paper now lay upon it. Lucy sat on the other side of the desk.

"Have a seat, lad," the Captain instructed, pointing to an empty chair opposite his daughter.

"Will you write something for me?"

Christopher picked up a quill, dipped it in ink, and started to write.

Good afternoon, Captain Hughes

"Good," the Captain said. "Very good."

Lucy smiled.

"Do you know what this is?" he asked, placing an instrument on the table. Christopher wrote:

Yes

"Tell me in what direction the boat is headed, " the Captain challenged. Christopher smiled. Leo had just taught him how to read a compass. Its arrow is magnetized and will always point north. Sailors started using compasses hundreds of years ago so they would know what direction they were sailing in, regardless of whether the sun was shining or not. Christopher held the compass in his hand. He gripped the quill.

Southwest

"I see Cookie was right. You are a bright young man. I do not know how your uncle failed to inform me of your capabilities."

A knock on the door distracted the Captain.

"Come in."

"Sir, Mr. Johnson would like a word with you," the sailor named Henry said. Christopher, Henry, and Henry's twin brother, Nathan, worked on the same watch. Only five years older than him, Henry had taught Christopher how to climb and maneuver between the heavy lines while aloft. The young man was almost better than Sugar herself at moving between ropes.

"Tell him I will be right there, Henry," the Captain said.

"Aye, aye, sir." Wisps of soft brown hair curled out from beneath Henry's navy blue knit cap.

The door closed and the Captain turned his back to them. "I'd better see what this is about. I will be back soon. Lucy, go through the rest of the things we talked about with Christopher so I can better assess his level of learning."

CHAPTER 39

The door shut behind the Captain.

"I didn't think we'd ever get another chance to talk," Lucy said. "Have you found out anything more?"

Christopher dragged his hand through his hair.

"I told you to leave things alone, Lucy. You have no idea the trouble you are in."

"I'm not very good with directions," she shrugged.

Christopher gave up. "No, I still don't have what I need." Christopher took a tattered piece of paper out of his shirt. "Here is a list of the sailors I suspect. There is one thing though." Christopher's mood brightened. "When I was taking food to the crew, I saw a pistol in one of the sailor's sea chests."

Lucy's eyebrows rose. "But the crew isn't allowed to have guns."

"Exactly."

"Did you see whose it was?"

"No."

Christopher slumped. Lucy sighed. Minutes passed before either of them talked again.

"Christopher, I know I this is going to sound crazy, but something strange happened after the storm."

Christopher's eyebrows rose. "Oh yeah?" Strange didn't even begin to cover half the things he had seen since boarding the Georgiana.

"There was a mouse on Sugar's back. He was about so big," Lucy said, spreading her index finger and thumb apart, "brown, and well . . . "

Christopher laughed through his nose. "He was talking?"

"Please tell me you saw him, too."

"Yes," Christopher said, opening the pouch hanging at his side. Leo crawled into his hand, and Christopher set him on the table.

Lucy blinked.

"Lucy, I would like to introduce you to Leo," Christopher said.

Leo stood on his back paws. "It is nice to meet you," said the mouse.

Lucy rubbed her eyes. "Did you hear that?"

"Of course," Christopher said. "Leo is my human guide, and he can talk."

CHAPTER 40

"Adults do not understand. Talking animals are beyond their comprehension," Leo said, warning Lucy. "They will think you are crazy. No good will come from it if you're thinking of telling them."

"I won't say a word," Lucy promised.

"Thank you," said Leo with a twitch of his whiskers.

The doorknob jiggled, and Leo darted back into Christopher's pouch.

"Hello, Papa," Lucy greeted. "Good afternoon, Mr. Johnson," she added, seeing that her father was no longer alone.

"How did the lessons go?" asked the Captain.

"Very well. Christopher is an excellent pupil."

The Captain reached behind Christopher's chair and grabbed several large rolls of paper.

"We're here to check on our bearings, children," he told them.

"Christopher?" Mr. Johnson asked as he was passed one of the large paper rolls. "Have you ever looked at a chart?" Christopher shook his head and approached the desk where the men stood. "A chart is a map of the sea."

Mr. Johnson unfurled the large roll of paper. Different colored markings littered its surface. Some images that looked like landmasses were dark brown while others held no color. Numbers written on wavelike lines covered the entire sheet.

"According to my recent calculations we should be entering Anagada Channel right about here. Our first indication that we are on course will be Sombrero Island, here." Christopher followed Mr. Johnson's hand as he pointed to the top of the chart and then down to a small black mark. "Anagada Island is much too low to be spotted from a distance. The reefs that surround her can be very dangerous, so we'll keep a wide berth if it is her shores we see first."

Mr. Johnson unrolled another chart. The Captain stood staring at the pictures laid out in front of him. His arms were crossed. He stroked his chin with his left hand. Deep wrinkles creased his forehead.

The door to the cabin opened. "Afternoon," Cookie greeted. The old man grinned from ear to ear. "I thought the children might be in need of a little nourishment and I also thought I'd warn you that the Admiral is on his way."

"The Admiral is well enough to leave his cabin?" asked the Captain.

"Aye, he thought it was high time he got some fresh

air. Been driving our poor Mr. Miller crazy, I think." The Captain groaned. "Some of the men have been saying we're getting close to land. Seen a sea bird myself just this morning."

"We are approximately a four-day sail from Tortola," Mr. Johnson confirmed, as Cookie placed the tray on the table.

"If the wind is cooperating, this evening we shall celebrate our successful crossing," the Captain said.

Cookie grinned. "I have enough supplies for a little party of sorts, if you are willing. The men have been working hard. The break will be good for morale."

The Captain nodded. "Make it so, Cookie."

Mr. Miller eased the British naval officer through the cabin door. He looked thin, his cheeks lacked color, and he did not seem as intimidating as he had before, Christopher thought.

"Good afternoon, gentlemen," Admiral Cunningham greeted.

"Afternoon," Mr. Johnson replied, helping the Admiral from Mr. Miller's arm to the chair.

"Thank you." The Admiral sat.

Cookie cleared his throat. "Well, if that be all for me, sir, I shall be heading back to the galley. I'll be needing you in a bit, Chris, so don't stay too long."

"Wait for me," Mr. Miller chimed in. "I'll see you

gentlemen at supper. I must head back and tidy up the infirmary."

The Admiral laughed and Christopher's mouth dropped. He had never seen the officer smile, let alone laugh. "Good man, that Mr. Miller," the Admiral complimented, much to the cabin's occupants' surprise.

Mr. Johnson turned back to the charts and continued explaining how to read them to Christopher.

The Admiral sat quietly in his chair leafing through a book. The second time the bells chimed, the Captain turned to Christopher and told him it was time to attend to his other duties.

"Captain," the Admiral announced as Christopher started to leave, "I think I shall excuse myself as well. The boy can escort me back to the infirmary."

Christopher offered the Admiral his arm, but he refused and instead got to his feet with the help of a cane the doctor had left. "Shall we?"

*

Boots leaned up against the guardrail outside of the Captain's cabin cleaning his nails with the end of his blade. He watched Christopher and the Admiral leave and then fell in step behind them.

"Christopher, I wanted to thank you," the Admiral said.

"Mr. Miller has told me that you saved my life. I know I have not been fair to you. I can be a judgmental old man, but I am happy to admit when I have made a mistake."

Christopher felt a pang of guilt for the bad feelings he had been harboring against the Admiral.

"Mr. Jones," the Admiral announced, stopping abruptly. He turned to face Boots, who stood a few feet behind him, and tapped his cane loudly against the deck. "Do you need something, or do you plan to escort us all the way to our destination?"

Boots jumped. "No, sir."

The Admiral huffed as Boots moved on.

"I do not like that uncle of yours. He is not the kind of man a boy like yourself deserves. I would like you to consider a position in the Navy when we are finished here, Christopher. I think you would make a fine officer."

CHAPTER 41

"Four days till land," Lucy muttered, pacing.

"Stop whispering, child," the Captain said, trying to concentrate on the business before him.

She needed to act. Lucy tugged on her father's arm. Christopher would not be happy with her decision, but it needed to be done. She would make her father understand. He needed to know the truth.

"I need to talk to you, Papa. It's important. Please."

The Captain glanced at his daughter. She was clearly upset. "Let me finish up with Mr. Johnson and I will be right there."

"Papa, please," Lucy asked again.

"It's alright, sir," Mr. Johnson replied. "I should be checking a few more things out on deck anyway."

"Thank you, Mr. Johnson."

Once Mr. Johnson had left, the Captain turned to Lucy.

"Now Lucy, what's this all about? I'm very busy at the moment. I don't appreciate the interruption."

"I'm sorry, Papa, but this concerns all of us."

"Okay," he told her, looking doubtful. "I'm all ears."

Lucy walked to the cabin door and checked that it was secure.

"Papa, it's about Christopher."

Chapter 42

The deck was filled with merriment by the time the officers had finished with their supper. Two men Christopher recognized from Boots' watch were singing, while another man who went by the name of Jack played a cheerful jig on his fiddle. Someone strung lanterns up in the low hanging rigging, and the deck was bathed in a warm glow.

The Captain and his officers left the table early and had already made it up onto the aft poop deck where they could watch the celebration taking place on the main deck below.

"Good night, Christopher," Lucy called after him as he left with the Captain's cabin with the supper dishes. "I'll see you tomorrow."

Christopher couldn't help waving back as he teetered through the men who danced on deck.

Looking up at the star-filled sky, Christopher could just make out Sugar's tail on the first main mast platform. He knew Leo would be with her watching the goings-on. He hoped they wouldn't get into any trouble and looked forward to the stories of the sailors they would bring back.

Christopher helped Cookie wash the last of the dishes.

"Up on deck with you now, young man," Cookie said finally as he put down his towel. "I've got myself a meeting with the Captain. Go enjoy the fun."

Christopher looked down. As much as he wanted to join the men up on deck, Boots and Stinky would be there, and they were sure to be drinking. They were nasty enough without liquor coursing through their veins, so Christopher had no desire to see them well into their cups.

Cookie saw the disappointed look on Christopher's face, guessing what the boy was thinking. "Ah, yes, your uncle. I don't know if I'd want to run into him either after he's been into the rum."

Christopher shrugged and picked up the book he had left on the counter.

CHAPTER 43

The moon was high and the stars were bright as Cookie made his way through the drunken sailors to the Captain's cabin.

Upon seeing Cookie cross the main deck, the Captain excused himself from the officers' company and followed his old friend into the sanctuary of his private quarters.

"Follow me," the Captain said. "I need to talk to you about our young friend." Lucy came out of her room and sat in a chair next to the two men.

"I was wondering when we'd be chatting." Cookie reached into his pocket and pulled out several small pieces of torn paper. "I believe this is your handwriting," he said to Lucy.

Lucy carefully laid the scraps on the table and pieced them together. Sitting in front of her was the note she had written to Christopher so many nights before when she discovered that he could speak.

"It was in my oven when I went to re-light her after the storm. I've kept it with me since then, knowing you'd be letting me know about it when the time was right for us to talk."

"Thank you, Cookie," Lucy said, staring down at the note.

"My love," the Captain sighed, "I think it's best you tell Cookie what you told me this afternoon."

Lucy talked for the better part of an hour. Her father had listened carefully to her earlier. They argued a little, and now he wanted to hear what Cookie had to say. If he believed in Christopher as Lucy did, so would he. It angered him that he was not told sooner, but if what Lucy said was true he could understand Christopher's reservations.

"They've told him they'll kill him, you, and me if he speaks to anyone," Lucy said to Cookie. I know he's doing his best, but I am worried that we're running out of time. He doesn't know I've told Papa. Cookie, please don't be mad at him."

"I've had my thoughts. Now I know they're confirmed. I've known people who don't speak before. My own cousin, in fact, clever as can be, but Christopher never struck me as one, not even from the start. His silence is too forced, and his other senses haven't made up for the loss."

Cookie turned to the Captain.

"Captain, I can vouch for the boy; I trust him as if he were my own. He ain't got a bad bone in his body. If he says those men are pirates, I believe him."

"My intuition tells me this as well. Your approval

confirms it." The Captain took a deep breath and clenched his hands together. He turned to Lucy, who was standing at his side. "I admire the boy's bravery, but he is, as you are my dear, just a child. You should have come to me before this."

"I know," she admitted. "But if you did not believe him, Christopher would be dead."

"Aye," Cookie agreed. "She has a point. I've seen the way the boy is treated. I am surprised he has survived this long."

"To bed with you now, Lucy. Cookie and I must talk."

"But Papa . . ."

"Don't argue with me, young lady. I will not put you or Christopher in any more danger."

Lucy stomped into her cabin and slammed the door behind her.

"Cookie," the Captain said, turning to his old friend, "please get Mr. Miller and Mr. Johnson, and see if the Admiral is awake. It's crucial they know what's going on."

CHAPTER 44

The Captain and his officers talked late into the night. "Stay with me a while longer," he whispered to Cookie as the other men left. "I have something I need you to do."

When Cookie finally left, he carried with him a roughly hand-drawn chart, a compass, a knife, and a small pistol—all of which he tucked into a leather satchel. The music outside had stopped, and only a few drunken men remained up on deck.

"Okay, boys, wrap it up!" Cookie announced. The bells tolled two. "Enough is enough, up you go!" Cookie nudged a sleeping man with his boot. "Time to clear out." Begrudgingly, the men started to leave.

Cookie strolled the deck looking for stragglers. Only the smallest skeleton crew remained on deck to man the lines. Cautiously he made his way to the second forward skiff on the port side. It was a small emergency boat, but it had a good sail and a solid hull. It will have to do, he thought, as he tucked his small package under the skiff's wooden seat.

Cookie made the trip from the galley to the skiff three more times that night. Each time he checked to make sure no one was watching, and when he was satisfied he was alone, he hid another bundle.

CHAPTER 45

The next morning, the Georgiana lazily hummed to life. Having gone to bed early, Christopher made it onto the deck before many of the other sailors. The sun warmed his back as it rose in the eastern sky. This was Christopher's favorite time of day.

Looking around the main deck, Christopher could see the remnants of the party from the night before; it was going to take a while to clean up. He reached for his bucket. He watched a lone bird fly overhead, circling the ship before disappearing from sight.

"That's odd," Christopher mumbled.

"What is?" Leo yawned, rubbing his eyes as he climbed to Christopher's shoulder.

"I could swear I just saw a hawk circle the ship."

Leo shivered. "Well, I know there is at least one species of hawk indigenous to the Caribbean, but they don't usually fly out this far. Are you sure?"

"I think so. I've seen hawks before. One of my father's friends had one he used for hunting. I've never forgotten it."

"I hope you're wrong," Leo replied looking up at the sky. "Hawks and mice are natural enemies. Even talking about them shivers me timbers, as Boots would say."

Christopher plunged his bucket into the ocean then tossed out a handful of sand to ready the deck for its morning scrub.

"'Tis a glorious morn'n," Stinky spat as he and Boots emerged from the forward cabin. An evil grin spread across his face, baring brown stumps of his rotting teeth. "The water's get'n bluer. I can almost smell land."

Boots yawned and stretched his gangly arms over his head. "Aye, me hearty, 'tis a glorious day indeed." He slapped Stinky on the back.

The sun was high and the deck was beginning to get hot underfoot when Cookie called to Christopher. "I've got a lot of work for you today," he said loudly enough for Boots and Stinky to overhear. "I don't know if you'll make it back up here before your lesson."

Boots snorted. "Take the scallywag. He's of little use topside when the weather be so fair."

When they reached the galley, Sugar leaped from Cookie's shoulder to a shelf above. "Take a look about, girl, and let me know if we're alone. A minute later Sugar returned.

"Chi, chi, chi."

"All right then. Chris, I'm going to be blunt. I've

been suspecting something for a long time now, but I've been waiting for you to come to me when you saw fit." Christopher paled. "The Captain called me to his cabin last night. He and Miss Lucy sat me down."

Cookie saw the boy start to shake.

"It's okay. You've got a lot of guts doing what you've done. But it's time to come clean. Come tell me what you know."

"Yes, sir," Christopher's voice cracked.

Cookie wrapped his arms around Christopher, pulling him into a giant bear hug. It was the first time he had been held since his parents died, and the contact made him feel as though he may weep.

"You're not alone any more, son," Cookie said into Christopher's ear, still clutching him tightly. "I have your back. Lucy did right by telling us. Don't be mad at her for what she's done. She knew you two were in over your heads. After she told us, we came up with a plan of sorts. It's not going to make you happy, but you don't have a say. It's what's got to be done."

Christopher nodded. He had already caused enough trouble and wished only to prove himself useful.

"Now, give me the list of sailors you showed Lucy. I need to know who you think has turned."

Cookie spread the list out on the counter. "Aye," he said at last, rubbing his finger across his chin. "I noticed them acting funny, too. I watched the last of the men from afar last night making a few observations of my own. Go fetch me the quill from my table in back."

"Tell him what else you saw this morning," Leo squeaked, following Christopher into the deserted room off the galley. "He may know what the hawk is doing way out here."

Christopher nodded.

"Here you are, sir," Christopher said.

"Now don't be getting all formal on me now that I know you can talk. I am Cookie to the crew, and I'll be offended if you call me anything else."

Christopher nodded.

"Is there anything else I should note?"

"I saw a hawk circling the rigging earlier today. It seemed funny to me seeing a bird like that so far from shore."

Cookies eyes widened. "A hawk, you say?"

"Yes."

"Well if that be true, we are in more danger than I thought."

"What do you mean?"

"Red Blade, one of the last known pirates in these waters, keeps just such a bird."

Leo bowed his head and Sugar screeched.

"Christopher, I want you to stay here until I tell you otherwise. There's plenty to do. Just make yourself busy. "

"Why?"

"The Captain and I have a couple things to take care of and I don't think it's safe for you up top right now. If Boots and Stinky sense something is different they'll know you've talked. We're getting close to land, and emotions will be running high. The safest thing to do is to keep you out of sight."

"But I can help!"

"Sorry, Chris, but if what you say is true, then we have to move fast. Last night when the deck finally cleared, the Captain had me provision the second port side skiff. When another ship is spotted on the horizon, a call will come from the lookout, so be ready. I want you and Lucy in that boat."

Christopher gripped the counter. "You can't be serious. I can help. I can't leave you after all that's happened."

"Listen to me. The Captain will create a diversion that should give us enough time to launch the skiff. I am to take you to the nearest island and drop you off. Then l will sail on to get help."

"What?" Christopher choked. "The Captain will be outnumbered. We can't just abandon him. They'll kill him!"

"Pirates in these parts usually don't kill their prisoners. If the Captain hands the boat over without a fight, the pirates will confiscate the ship. Then they'll hold the

Captain and any other sailors loyal to him for ransom. That won't happen if Lucy's onboard and the Captain is compromised. They'll see she's his weakness and ask for more. He needs you to help me get her out of here."

Chapter 46

Christopher had not seen the horizon since morning. At 4:00 p.m., the first watch came down to supper.

When the last sailor in the first watch finished eating and headed back up on deck, Cookie took Christopher into the storeroom.

"Grab whatever you think you might need from your cabin. You probably won't be returning to it again. Then I'll be having you take this food to the Captain's cabin. I want you to stay there. Mr. Johnson and Mr. Miller will be in the cabin as well. They have all been told what's been going on. They are good men. The Captain knows them well. They have been loyal sailors for years and have sworn to stay onboard to help."

Christopher nodded then made his way through the deserted mess hall back to his tiny cabin.

"I saw the hawk thrice today. The Dragon's Breath is near. Red Blade will be wait'n to attack when the sun goes down. He'll be count'n on a quick takeover. Do we have what we need?" Boots said from inside the cabin.

"Aye," another replied.

"Here's the key to the gun locker. Get the guns and meet me in the forecastle when the second watch finishes their sup."

"I thought I'd be grab'n the guns?" Stinky snorted, enraged.

"No!" Boots snapped. "Yer gonna head to the infirmary and take care of the Admiral for us. If there's one thing that don't belong onboard when Red Blade arrives, it's a naval officer."

Christopher backed away from the door and sprinted back into the empty galley, his heart thudding against his rib cage.

"Cookie?"

"Watch your voice, son," Cookie reprimanded. "The second watch is due in a few minutes."

Christopher grabbed Cookie's arm and dragged him to a safe corner where they could talk.

"I see," Cookie said upon hearing the news. "We'll move the Admiral to the Captain's cabin as well. Stay here and help me serve until I return, then gather up the Captain's meal and be on your way."

Christopher slid his apron over his head. The bell had yet to ring, but already a line was forming. From the far side of the mess hall, Christopher watched Boots and Stinky approach. Boots cut to the front of the line.

"If the food be warm, ye best be serv'n us now, boy. We

got things to do." Christopher grabbed a towel and went to check the oven. "Get a move on before we decide it's ye we want to eat, not this tired old slop Cookie be giv'n us. Extra rations of meat here for me friends."

The other crewmen in line cheered.

CHAPTER 47

Christopher exhaled when he saw that the Admiral was already seated in the Captain's cabin. He did not know if he should say hello or remain silent so he just set food on the sideboard and started setting the dining table.

The Admiral, the Captain, and Mr. Miller were discussing the charts sprawled across the desk, and Mr. Johnson and Lucy were talking next to the bookcases.

"It seems we underestimated you, young man," the Captain said, approaching the dining table. Christopher stiffened and dropped a fork, sending it clanging to the ground.

Lucy rushed to his side. "Christopher, forgive me. I had to tell them."

"I know," he said bowing his head. "I should have done it myself."

The Captain gripped the boy's shoulder. "Your deception was forced upon you. We owe you our thanks, not condemnation."

"I am sorry," Christopher said to the room.

The Admiral, who stood silently until now, spoke.

"Young man, I am used to saving lives, not having mine saved. It seems that you have now done it twice."

Christopher blushed.

"To think of what you've been through on my own ship infuriates me!" the Captain roared, pounding his fist on the table. The room stilled. The Captain took a deep breath. "Christopher," he said, pacing to the other side of the cabin, "thanks to you we still have the element of surprise on our side. I am assuming that Cookie has talked to you and that you have agreed to help me get Lucy to safety?"

"Yes, sir."

Lucy looked surprised. "Papa?"

"It is for the best. If you are here, the pirates will use you against me."

A single tear rolled down Lucy's cheek.

"When the call comes from the lookout that another boat is approaching, you have to get to the skiff Cookie prepared. There won't be a second to spare, do you understand? You must get off this ship as soon as possible."

"But Papa!"

"Enough!"

The tension in the room was only broken seconds later with a knock on the door and a rattle of the latch to the cabin.

"Hope you're hungry," Cookie said, carrying more food and with Sugar following at his feet.

The Captain exhaled loudly. "Is everything in order?"

"Aye, sir," Cookie answered.

"And the other item?"

"I took care of that early this morning. The King's guns are still where they ought to be, but the ammunition and powder are hidden. I am the only one who knows where they are. If those sea rats try and get the location out of you or anyone else in this room, you can truthfully reply that you haven't got a clue."

"Good job. Mr. Johnson?"

"Captain?"

"Have you talked to our man yet?"

"Mr. Bruce is on watch in the lookout. He has agreed to help."

"How do we know we can trust him?" asked the Admiral.

The Captain looked at Mr. Johnson.

"He's my cousin," Mr. Johnson answered. "We keep our alliances quiet on the ship so it doesn't interfere with our work. He will alert us when he spots something and then pretend to turn pirate with the other men. If worse comes to worst, and we do not hear from Cookie, he will escape and lead the Navy to the guns."

"Well?" Cookie interrupted. "Shall we all sit down and eat?"

"Yes," the Captain agreed. "A warm meal is exactly what we all need right now."

Christopher glanced at the men seated around the table. When no one was watching, he slipped a few tasty bites into his pouch for Leo.

Less than an hour later came another knock on the door.

The Captain put his napkin down on the table and nodded. This was it, he feared, and silently prayed that everything would go as he planned.

He squeezed Lucy's shoulder as he stood. He would be fine once he was sure she was safely off the ship.

"Come in," he ordered.

It was Mr. Bruce. "Captain, there's something you better be seeing."

As Christopher reached the door they heard the call from the lookout.

"Ship ahoy!"

CHAPTER 48

"Who is she? What flag does she fly?" the Captain demanded as he exited the cabin.

The children had one shot to escape. They couldn't afford to take any risks. Cookie held Lucy and Christopher at the door to the Captain's parlor while Mr. Bruce stood next to the Captain on the deck looking out at the approaching vessel.

The first signs of dusk brushed the evening sky. The slightest breeze rustled through the rigging, eight to ten knots at the most—not quite enough for a heavy ship like the Georgiana, but if they were lucky it would be perfect for the small sail on the skiff.

"She's flying a British flag, Captain," a man in the rigging called out, pointing to starboard.

The Captain approached the rail and extended his spyglass.

"Admiral?" the Captain said, spying the ship.

He passed the glass to the naval officer, who shook his head upon seeing the ship. "There are no ships in the Royal Fleet with a red hull, Captain."

The Captain sighed. "I thought not."

Mr. Johnson turned the Georgiana to port and the crew crowded the starboard rail, fighting for a glimpse of the approaching warship.

"Mr. Bruce, lower a skiff to be used as an emissary," the Captain ordered. He bent down and kissed Lucy on the forehead. "This is it, my dear. Remember what I've told you."

Lucy choked back tears. "I love you."

"I love you, too."

"Chris," Cookie whispered, "get to the skiff. I'll meet you as soon as I can."

Christopher reached for Lucy. "Ready?"

Lucy nodded and rested her hand in his. Together they hurried past the sailors, whose backs were turned to the bow. When they reached the foremast, they saw Mr. Bruce and the twins, Henry and Nathan, position the skiff over the rail.

Sugar screeched as a breathless Cookie joined them in the lee of the foremast. With a final heave, the skiff locked into place and Mr. Bruce dismissed the twins.

"Quickly, children," Mr. Bruce advised.

Cookie crawled beneath the canvas sail covering the open skiff and reached for Lucy.

"You're a good lad," Mr. Bruce said, helping Christopher aboard. He held out his hand, passing Christopher a worn leather case.

"Hurry, Chris!" Cookie called.

"Thank you, sir," Christopher said to Mr. Bruce as he accepted the package.

Mr. Bruce's eyes locked on his. "Be careful."

As soon as the canvas covered Christopher, Mr. Bruce lowered the skiff to the water.

"Stay low," Cookie instructed. "Don't make a sound."

Christopher felt Lucy's heart beating as she pressed against him.

Mr. Bruce watched the small skiff float away. As soon as it was free of the Georgiana, he went back to the poop deck to update the Captain.

"All hands men!" the Captain called, watching his daughter drift farther from the ship. "I have changed my mind. Take in the top sails and come about, let us sail out to greet them."

The more distance the Captain could put between the Georgiana and the skiff, the better. With a little luck, the skiff would soon be forgotten.

Chapter 49

Boots couldn't believe it. The Captain was welcoming the Dragon's Breath. What a dolt! Sailors rushed about the deck securing sails. The Georgiana changed her course.

The fire of the setting sun danced across the faces of the sailors. In the distance the Captain saw traces of disorderly naval uniforms running around on the deck of the approaching vessel.

As the ship drew nearer, the men onboard her howled. A warning shot fired across the bow of the Georgiana and a sailor in the crow's nest took down the Union Jack and hoisted the Skull and Crossbones in its place.

Captain Hughes looked over his shoulder. The skiff was but a speck on the horizon. A second warning shot roared across his bow, shaking the deck.

"Now!" Boots screamed to his mutinous men. Pulling his saber from its scabbard, he charged the aft deck.

The officers and a few loyal seamen circled the Captain.

"Quarter!" the Captain yelled raising his hands into the air. "Stand down men. I will not have your blood on my hands."

Boots snarled. "If that be so, I be take'n yer ship."

Boots seized the wheel. His hands caressed the worn wooden spires and half his face turned up in a smile. He turned the Georgiana into the wind, luffing the sails. "Stinky!" he shouted. "Lock these scurvy dogs below. Make sure the girl and Cookie be with them. Then get that useless excuse of a boy up on deck. I want him be stand'n next to me so Red Blade sees what else I brung 'em. "

"Aye, sir," Stinky replied pushing the barrel of his pistol into the Captain's back. "This way!"

Chapter 50

As the Dragon's Breath drew near, the men onboard her threw their grappling hooks. The Georgiana bucked as the Dragon's Breath secured her to its side.

From his cabin below, Captain Hughes cursed as he watched the pirates stretch a plank between the two ships and a boarding party rush his deck.

Stinky ran up to Boots' side. "Boots," he whispered, panting. "Boots . . ."

"What is it ye dolt? Can't ye see I be busy?" Boots straightened his coat and checked his appearance in the reflection of his saber's polished blade.

"The boy!" Stinky hunched over, resting his hands on his knees. He took two big gulps of air. "I can't find the boy, the girl, or the pesky old cook."

"What?"

"They be gone, Boots. Port side skiff, too."

Boots grabbed Stinky by the scruff of his neck. "Speak not another word and say noth'n of this to another soul!" he threatened. "Ain't nothin' that old cod and them two worthless brats can do to us anyhow."

A hawk cry pierced the air. With two giant pulls from its powerful wings, it landed on the massive shoulders of its master.

"Good girl," a menacing deep voice cooed while placing a tiny leather hood over the bird's powerful head. The rings on the man's fingers reflected the intensity of the sun's final moments on the horizon, with the red sky matching the rubies set within three of the seven bands he wore. From the man's left ear hung a feather matching his hawk's on a golden hoop. His long, soot-colored beard reached his waist, braided in places with beads made of bone tied to the ends.

The boards creaked as he stepped onto the ramp connecting his ship to the one he just acquired. The men before him cheered and dipped their heads as he passed. A gust of wind caught his blood-splattered, black dress coat, pushing it open. He always wore black. The color calmed him.

The boarding party moved aside as Boots stepped forward. "Cap'n," he bowed, "the Georgiana." Boots swept his hand in front of him.

Red Blade's eyes scanned the ship from beneath his tricon hat.

"Men!" he thundered. "Find me the guns!"

A dozen of the sailors that had crossed to the Georgiana with him disappeared below deck and within minutes

returned carrying a dozen large wooden crates branded with the King's seal.

"Shall we have a look?" Red Blade snarled.

The pirates cheered while several shot their pistols into the air.

The man on Red Blade's right took out his dagger and knelt down next to the first crate.

"Open them!" Red Blade ordered. One by one, the crate tops were pried wide open, their contents inspected, and then placed on the deck.

Over three hundred flintlock pistols and another two hundred Brown Bess muskets lay at their feet.

"Is that all?" Red Blade demanded. The crew looked confused. There were more weapons than they had hoped for.

Boots looked startled. "Cap'n?"

Red Blade's cheeks flushed with anger.

"I see guns, but no gun powder and no shot. What good are these weapons if we have nothing to put in them?" he asked.

Boots started to answer, then stopped. He had been so thorough, so sure. He had never even considered the possibility of an incomplete cargo.

Red Blade pulled one of four pistols from his shoulder belt and checked to see if the barrel was loaded.

"Where is the Captain of the Georgiana now?" Red

Blade asked, the veins on the side of his head beginning to bulge.

Boots' finger shook as he pointed to the door on the far side of the deck. "In there, sir. Locked in his cabin with the others who have refused to join us."

"Others?" Captain Red Blade stroked his beard. He would have the guns and the gunpowder if it were the last thing he did.

"How many men?"

"Eight, sir, including the Captain and a British Admiral," Boots replied.

"An Admiral?"

"Aye, sir."

"Bring them to me!"

CHAPTER 51

The sea of men parted as Captain Hughes and his loyal followers were pushed through.

Red Blade ran a calloused hand down his hawk's back before removing her hood. "Fly!"

With a nod she flew to the yardarm above.

"I have a problem," Red Blade announced. "I have guns but no gunpowder or shot. Even your ship's gun stores seem to have run dry. You are either the most unprepared Captain to sail these waters or the stupidest."

"My ship is not known for her speed," Captain Hughes replied evenly. "She is a merchant vessel that has been claimed by the crown to transport a shipment of weapons. My men were not told of this cargo. It was loaded at night, in secret, back in England. I have not inspected the cargo, nor have I embraced the idea of such a shipment aboard my vessel. As for your comment regarding my ship's big guns, I do not carry gunpowder because I know her limits. Defending her would only mean death for everyone onboard. I would rather surrender my goods than risk losing a man."

Red Blade placed his enormous hand on Captain Hughes' shoulder, forcing him to his knees. The Captain winced. Red Blade pressed the tip of his pistol into the Captain's brow. The cold steel against his skin sent a ripple of fear down the Captain's spine and he started to sweat.

"The powder was to be shipped a fortnight hence aboard another ship," the Admiral blurted, stepping out from behind the other prisoners.

Red Blade glanced at the man's uniform. The naval officer was thin and held a cane, but his arrogant expression told Red Blade all he needed to know. The Admiral would be enough to secure a sizable ransom. Maybe all was not lost.

Red Blade growled, "We shall see." He released the Captain and holstered his pistol. "You had better pray that your story rings true, or it will be your flesh my bird dines on tonight!"

Mr. Johnson and Mr. Miller helped the Captain to his feet.

"Load the guns onto the Dragon's Breath!" Red Blade ordered. Once we're at anchor I'll send the Navy word of our guests. Several barrels of gunpowder seem a fair price for a few men's lives."

Red Blade stepped back aboard the Dragon's Breath. They would be at their safe harbor by morning. With any luck, Red Blade would have his ammunition within a fortnight.

CHAPTER 52

Minutes passed like hours under the thick canvas sail.

"Cookie," Lucy pleaded. "I'm not feeling very well. I can't breathe."

"Patience, dear," Cookie answered. "It wont be long now."

Leo squirmed from his pouch and crawled toward the flap of the sail at the back of the small dory, pushing it aside. His ear perked and his pink nose twitched.

"It's safe to remove the sail now," Leo whispered when he returned to Christopher.

"Cookie," Christopher said. "Can we lift the sail a bit and get some air? I feel as though I may be sick as well."

Cookie raised the canvas corner closest to him. Lucy coughed as fresh air filled the boat. "Just keep your heads down."

Christopher closed his eyes.

"The currents and wind are in our favor," Cookie said, peering over the railing. "Once it gets dark we'll hoist the sail and make for land."

Christopher patted his shirt and took out the worn leather pouch he had tucked into it earlier. Unwrapping the cord that kept it bound, Christopher was stunned to see Mr. Bruce's treasured spyglass fall into his hands. He brushed his fingers down its length.

Cookie wrestled with the sail while he searched for one of the barrels of fresh water and a cup to pass around.

"Where on earth did you come by that?" Cookie asked.

"Mr. Bruce passed it to me as we boarded the skiff."

"Well then, Chris, be honored. I've never known the man not to have it in his possession. It was his father's, and his father's father before that. You must have made quite an impression on him."

Christopher extended the spyglass as Mr. Bruce had done days before in the crow's nest. Cautiously he raised his head above the rail and pointed the glass in the direction of the Georgiana.

"Papa," Lucy whispered, holding her breath as Christopher looked.

Cookie patted her hand. "Now, now, Miss Lucy, I've seen your dad come through worse scrapes than this. Don't you worry."

Guilt surged through Christopher. The Captain was in even more danger now and he couldn't help feeling that somehow it was his fault.

The sun dipped below the horizon.

CHAPTER 53

As soon as it was dark, the tiny skiff hoisted her sail. The wind was coming from behind them and the sailing conditions were perfect. In no time they were speeding across the gently rolling seas.

"At this speed we'll make land by sunrise," Cookie announced.

Moonlight lit up the skiff making it easy to see. He double-checked the compass to make sure his bearings were correct.

Lucy curled up on the floor of the skiff, which was made of several damp planks. Although it was a beautiful night to be out on the water, she wished she were safely tucked into her own cabin. Christopher grabbed one of the wool blankets Cookie had packed and laid it over her.

"Thank you," she mumbled.

"Chris," Cookie said, "try and get some sleep, too. I'll wake you in a few hours and have you take the tiller so that I can do the same. I'm not sure what tomorrow may bring, but I know we'll need all the energy we can muster."

Christopher grabbed a blanket and lay down on the floor next to Lucy.

"It will be okay," Leo comforted. "You'll see. The Captain is a smart man. He knew what he was doing."

*

"Time to wake up, son," Cookie said, gently shaking Christopher. Bright stars danced across an endless sky.

"Have you ever sailed a boat like this before?" Cookie asked.

"No," Christopher answered honestly. "But I've watched you, and I've read about it."

"Well then you should be fine. It's really quite easy, not much different than a bigger boat. Sit here. Now take the tiller in your hand. Push the tiller away from you to turn to starboard. Then pull the tiller toward you to turn to port. Adjust the sails so that they are always full, but make sure the boat isn't heeling too much on one side or the other. The compass is here. Keep heading west and we'll reach land eventually. Now have a seat and get a feel for the way she moves."

Christopher smiled and rubbed the sleep from his eyes. He learned quickly how to maneuver her through the water and liked the way the skiff responded to his touch. Waves lapped against the hull. The sails luffed when he released the main sheet, then filled again when he pulled it in.

"Good enough," Cookie said, when he was satisfied. "Wake me if the wind changes direction."

Christopher looked down at the compass and then across the starry horizon.

"You are doing well," Leo squeaked when Cookie began to snore.

Sailing the small boat felt like nothing Christopher had ever done before. It was exhilarating. He listened to every sound and felt every wave as it pushed them closer to their destination.

Lucy stirred. She got a chill when she realized Christopher was no longer next to her.

"Hey," he whispered, seeing her sit up. Lucy glanced over at Cookie sleeping in the bow, Sugar wrapped in his arms.

"How long has he been asleep?"

"Not long, an hour maybe."

Lucy moved next to him. "It's beautiful out here."

Christopher nodded. "How are you?"

"Better," she said, leaning into his side. Christopher adjusted his blanket so it covered them both.

Leo started to whistle an old sea tune that Lucy recognized from her childhood. She could barely hear it over the wind, but it soothed her.

The sun was just starting to come up over the horizon when Christopher woke Cookie.

"Lucy," he whispered, nudging her. "Look."

In the distance, off the starboard side of the bow stood the dark purple outline of an island.

CHAPTER 54

By the time the sun was high in the sky, they were sailing along the coastline of the island.

"Do you know where we are?" Lucy asked as Cookie fiddled with his roughly drawn chart.

"To tell the truth, Miss Lucy, I'm not exactly sure," the old man confessed. "When we left the Georgiana we were approximately here." Cookie placed his forefinger in the middle of the paper. "Currents have been pushing us in this direction and the winds been coming from the southeast." Cookie let his finger drift left, and then down. "I believe we're right about here." He 'paused, and then added, "Let's sail around this next point. If I'm right, there should be a wee bay in there with waters too shallow for a big ship to come in."

Sure enough as they rounded the corner, sand as white as one of Master Sven's new silk shirts gave way to lush green trees with leaves the size of Christopher's head. Tall cliffs wrapped the bay on all sides isolating the beach from the rest of the island.

"Bring in the sail," Cookie said. "We'll row from here."

He picked his way through the sharp coral heads fifty feet from shore.

The solid unmoving land beneath Christopher's feet felt foreign to him and he stumbled as he leapt from the boat.

"You should be safe here," Cookie said. "Make your camp in those gumbo trees. You'll be able to see out in case someone sails by, but no one will be able to see in."

Yellow-breasted birds darted between the treetops.

"I shouldn't be gone long, but it will be safer for you here on land than with me on the water."

Lucy and Christopher nodded.

"I've left you the supplies you'll need to get by: a net for fishing, a flint to start fires, and you know what fruits to eat, Lucy."

"I do."

"Fresh drinking water will be your biggest worry." Cookie grabbed several banana tree leaves. "The barrel I'm leaving you should keep you a couple days, if you're careful, but after that you'll be needing to start a collection. Set the leaves out when you see the clouds coming and you should be able to gather enough rain to get by."

When the old man was certain they knew what needed to be done, he headed back to the boat.

"I'll be leaving Sugar with you. Remember to hide if she

starts to shriek." Cookie untied her pink bow and placed her in Lucy's arms. "Don't look so worried, you two. This skiff here is made from sturdy English Oak. She's strong as an ox. I'll be back to get you in no time."

"I hope he's right," Christopher said as they watched Cookie row out into the open water and set sail.

The water lapped at Lucy's feet.

"So do I."

CHAPTER 55

The nonstop shuffle of curious lizards and hermit crabs prevented a good night's sleep, and the sand fleas that had invaded their camp during the night left Christopher and Lucy itching at the tiny red welts that now covered their entire bodies.

"This is ridiculous!" Leo complained, as Sugar helped pick the bugs from his fur. "We have to build some kind of platform to sleep on tonight or we will all go insane."

Christopher looked at the two sea bags Cookie had left, which he had yet to go through.

Sugar clucked and tugged at the cord of the first bag. "Okay, girl, settle down," Christopher said, helping the monkey open the bag. Inside, Christopher discovered a pair of short pants, a white cotton shirt, and a dark brown leather tie with a pouch attached. Christopher smiled as he remembered a similar pile that had been left for him once.

"I think these are meant for you," he said, handing the package to Lucy.

Lucy covered her mouth as she examined the clothing.

She had never worn pants before. It just wasn't proper; her mother would die if she found out.

"Are you sure?"

Christopher nodded.

"Okay then. Sugar, make sure the boys keep their backs turned."

Lucy ducked behind a bush. The feel of fabric surrounding her legs was incredible. It felt amazing to move around with such ease and not worry about her dress snaring in a bramble. What freedom, she thought, rubbing her hands down her thighs. She should have been born a boy.

"What do you think?" she said, popping into the clearing.

"Very nice." Christopher grinned.

"Are you laughing at me?"

Christopher snorted and then tried to make a serious face. "No."

"Yes, you are!"

"It's just . . . you look a bit like me, with brown hair and eyes is all."

"I most certainly do not!"

Christopher stood, walked around Lucy, and stood at her side. Sure enough, their legs matched in length, both their tangled locks were tied back from their faces, and sun-kissed freckles darted across their cheeks and noses.

"You've grown," Lucy huffed. "I was taller than you when you boarded the Georgiana." Christopher's brow raised. "It's true! Don't deny it!"

"I don't,"Christopher said with a smirk and then cleared his throat. His voice had gotten deeper and his muscles more defined, but Lucy would not mention those aloud, for the information would go straight to his head and there would be no living with him for the next couple days.

"Personally, I don't care what you think. I am more than happy to be done with that thing." Lucy pointed to the heap of dirty white fabric in the sand. "If you wish, you may give it a whirl."

Christopher's face squished together. Lucy looked at his pants then down at the brown pants she wore. They were darker than Christopher's but similar in style.

"Now there's just one more thing I need if I'm supposed to look like you." Lucy removed a small scabbard spilling out from the open bag and tucked it into the pouch she wore.

Christopher smiled. "Perfect."

Hands on hips, Lucy proudly posed. "Thank you."

Christopher bowed. "Anything for you, my lady." He took her hand and kissed it in jest.

"Okay, you two," Leo interrupted. "The sun's up, and there's work to do."

"Right," Christopher mumbled, heading back to the open bag in the sand. Digging into the canvas, Christopher found a length of rope and a hacksaw.

CHAPTER 56

By mid-morning their new platform was complete. It stood several feet above the sand and was surrounded by thick, low-lying, thorny bushes on three sides. Lucy designed, and with Sugar's help, they built a tightly woven palm frond roof to protect them from the weather with a shallow trough for collecting the rainwater. Thank goodness her nanny had taught her how to weave; all those afternoons making baskets for her mother had paid off. Clapping her hands together, she assessed their new camp.

Christopher approached her, fish in hand. "Well done," he complimented, dropping their meal onto a pile of clean banana leaves. He started a fire and together he and Lucy roasted his catch. Sugar chattered while passing them each a mango.

With bellies full, they lounged on the sand at the water's edge. The tall cliffs surrounding the camp seemed to reach the sky. "What do you think is on the other side of those peaks?" Christopher wondered out loud. Lucy shrugged.

Leo scampered onto Christopher's chest. "I think we should find out."

With a sigh Christopher pulled to his elbows. "I suppose you're right."

"Since Sugar and I are smaller," said Leo, "I think it would be beneficial for us to explore the caves on the bluff while you and Lucy get a good look at what's around us from the top of the hill."

Christopher poked Lucy.

"Sounds good to me," she said pushing up to her feet. "I'll race you up."

A hermit crab living in shells bigger than Christopher's fist scurried across the rocks in front of them and startled Christopher.

"Is Antigua like this?" he asked, breathing heavily.

Lucy's shoulders shook in silent laughter. "Yes, but my sisters aren't nearly as jumpy."

"Laugh all you want, but if you don't grow up with this it seems rather daunting."

When they reached the top, Christopher made for the shade of a lone tree. Embarrassed, he sat and closed his eyes briefly. When he reopened them he saw Lucy's jaw drop.

Her voice shook. "Christopher, what's that?"

A ribbon of smoke curled up from the bay two over from theirs. Christopher pulled out Mr. Bruce's spyglass.

"Lucy," he replied hesitantly, "I don't think we're the only ones on this island."

CHAPTER 57

"Well it's about time!" Leo chastised, as Christopher and Lucy ran into camp just after dusk. "We've been worried."

"Sorry," Christopher panted. Leo stood on his hind legs, tapping his paw on the sand.

"Leo," Christopher said, catching his breath, "we're not alone on the island."

Leo's ears stood on end. "What do you mean?"

"From the top of the hill Lucy spotted a campfire."

"Are you sure?" he questioned.

"Yes, there were several masts in the bay too."

"Could you see the ships?"

"No, not from where we were. The bay is not too far away though. I think we could walk there in an hour or so."

"Okay," Leo said. He was now pacing with his paws clasped behind his back.

"First, we need to find out who it is. Second, we need to make sure they don't see us. Christopher, scratch your footprints off the beach. Lucy, do the same around the camp. We need to make sure everything is out of sight. And everyone? No fires! At least until we know what we are up against."

Christopher smothered their campfire with sand and headed down toward the beach to do as Leo instructed. When he returned Leo was gone.

"Where did he go?" he asked Lucy. Sugar was curled into a ball and resting peacefully in her lap.

"I don't know," Lucy said and shrugged. "Come get some rest."

Christopher kicked the shrub closest to him before crawling into the lean tube next to Lucy.

"Don't worry. He'll be back soon," Lucy reassured, leaning against him.

The air next to Christopher whooshed as something fast and black darted past his head.

Lucy screamed. "What was that?"

"Don't panic," Leo squeaked, pulling himself onto the platform. "That is Ricardo and he is here to help."

A bat, not much larger than himself, landed next to Leo. He stretched his leathery wings out to the side then wrapped them around his body like a coat.

"When Sugar and I were in the caves earlier," Leo started, "we ran into a colony of Jamaican fruit bats. They were a very accommodating bunch, extremely friendly; Ricardo is their leader and he said he'd be happy to help us."

Ricardo screeched and bobbed his head. His black beady eyes reflected the moonlight filtering between the palm trees.

Leo grinned. "Tonight after his troop has eaten he promised to fly over to the bay for us and take a look."

CHAPTER 58

Sugar and Leo climbed the tallest fern tree near the shelter and waited for Ricardo to return while Christopher and Lucy slept.

"Ja, mon!" Ricardo called, soaring across the starlit sky. Looking at the height of the moon on the horizon Leo guessed it was still early yet, midnight at the latest.

"I be back, just like I said I would, and looky at what I bring ju. Dis is Isabella, da cute little she-bat I be telling you about dat lives in dat bay."

Isabella giggled.

"Hello," Leo greeted, bowing deeply.

Isabella batted her eyes.

"Don't ju be flirt'n with me girl," Ricardo said with a laugh and slapped Leo on the back. "She be me little mango blossom."

Isabella blushed as Ricardo kissed her cheek.

"Now like I be say'n, ju bay be a busy place. Dey be dree big floating man islands hanging out in da middle of da bay. One of dem be smaller den da others. Dat one been dare for days now, den one of dem big man islands be as red and ripe as me favorite berries. De dird big man island be new to da bay. No one ain't ever seen dat one before."

"Mmm hmm," Isabella nodded.

"Most of de floating man islands be empty right now. I see no humans walking upon them. Da humans all been rowing dem smaller floating islands to da beach," Ricardo continued.

"Dey got a big ol' fire going on in dare. I see a bunch of happy humans dare by dat fire. Dey all be singing and dancing. Dey be drinking out of big brown jugs making less sense as de night goes by.

"Now Isabella here she told me dere's dis big ugly bird dat be terrorizing all de colony. De bird be friends with da most uptight of all de humans. Dis man he never smile. He dressed all in black, black as night, and he be much taller den 'dem odder humans too."

Leo's eyes bulged and Sugar dropped the prickly pear she had been munching.

"Were there other men besides the ones that were singing? Men who were not as happy? Did one of them maybe have on a funny dark blue uniform?"

"Leo, mon, I be dere only a little while. Ju be hav'n to ask da fair Isabella now. Dat why I bring her back with me. She and her colony been living out in dat bay for years."

Leo turned to Isabella. "Isabella, please, do you think you've seen these sad men?"

"Ja," she said. "I see dese men you talk bout, da ones who don't sing. Dey be in our cave. Dey be strung up in some kind of funny looking net. Hung by da ceiling so dat no one can get out. Da singing men don't like da hanging men much. Dey yell at dem, treat dem cruel like."

"How many men are in your cave, Isabella?" Leo asked eagerly.

"Well now," she said, tapping her nail to her lip, "dare be at least four men tied up in de net and a few more locked up out on de newest of de float'n islands. Den dey be two men who sit just outside de cave by a small fire look'n all serious. Da men by da fire have knives and exploding sticks dat dey aim at me family. Dey do not like us very much I dink.

"Sometimes da man with da bird comes in to talk to da men in da net. I don't like dis bird. Da man he be out on da big red man island tonight. Da bird be out flying dough, out hunting most likely. Dey not drink'n with da odders."

"Ricardo, Isabella," Leo said, "will you and your colonies help us again? We have to get to the cave and see if the men that are hung up in the net are the men we know. If it is them, one of the men is the father of the human girl who sleeps below."

"Ja, of course we will," Ricardo assured. "We bats, we love to help you! Dis be fun!"

CHAPTER 59

"Christopher!" Leo yelled, scurrying down the fern tree as fast as his little legs would carry him. "Wake up!" He jumped onto Christopher's chest. "Christopher!"

"What?" the boy moaned sleepily. "Is it morning already?"

Christopher rubbed his eyes and wondered why it was still dark out.

"It's Red Blade!"

"What?" Christopher said, waking instantly. "Are you sure?"

"No, but if we leave now we can go get a look for ourselves before the sun comes up."

"Lucy!" Christopher yelled while grabbing her shoulder.

CHAPTER 60

It took just over an hour to reach the brush surrounding the outskirts of the pirates' camp.

They counted twenty-five men lounging around the fire in the cleared area away from the water. The pirate's cove was different from theirs as the cliff directly cut off the back of their camp, allowing it to wind deeper in to the brush before rising into the mountain's side. Most men were snoring; the rum in the brown jugs Ricardo mentioned had gotten the best of them. One man slumped against a tree singing to the moon in a drunken stupor. A couple of men gambled, wagering trinkets won in previous battles. Three others sat around the flames boasting of past battles.

"It's them!" Christopher whispered excitedly as he pulled out his spyglass. "Look, over there," Christopher pointed to the far side of the camp. He passed the spyglass to Lucy. Hidden behind trees was the guarded entrance to a cave. Leo and Sugar scrambled up a nearby tree to get a better look.

"That's it! It's got to be. I'll bet my tail that's where they've got the Captain," Leo squeaked.

Through the spyglass, Lucy saw two men huddled by a small fire outside of the opening just as Isabella had described according to Leo's account.

"Christopher, take Lucy and Sugar with you and make your way around the camp to the cave. I will meet you by the rocks on the right side of the opening. I'm going to get a quick look at what we're up against. And be careful," Leo cautioned. "Move slowly and cover your tracks. We don't want anyone to know we've been here."

Christopher nodded and motioned for Lucy and Sugar to follow him.

Leo kept low, scurrying between random objects scattered around the large campfire.

He added fifteen more men to the count they had made earlier, bringing the total number of pirates to forty.

Five large eight-man skiffs had been pulled up onto the beach. Leo wondered how many more sailors were left. He searched the bay for any other signs of life.

Overhead, a single hawk's cry cut through the night air.

CHAPTER 61

"Do you see Leo?" Christopher asked Lucy and Sugar as they all checked the bushes after reaching the area around the cave where they had agreed to meet.

Several large boulders and thick-thorned berry shrubs hid them from sight.

Christopher peered around the largest of the rocks. "He should be here. Do you think he already went in?"

Sugar chattered softly as she leapt into the nearest tree and crawled onto the limb that hung in front of the cave's entrance. As she walked across it, the branch swayed and several small leaves fell to the ground.

"Blimey!" a surprised guard yelled, spotting Sugar in the tree above his head. He raised his tankard to the sight, wavering under the weight of the drink.

"I hate them primates," the man next to him spat, swigging from the jug clutched in his hand. His lips curled revealing a mouth full of blackened gums.

"Shoot it!"

The first guard groped for his gun.

"Eep!" Sugar screeched, dashing from view.

The second guard barked a laugh. "Ye be too late!"

Placing his weapon back in its holster, the first guard cursed, "Damn monkey."

"Aye, barnacles on a beach," the second guard agreed, raising his jug.

The first guard sneered. "Crabs in yer boots."

Lucy blanched. Christopher raised his finger to his lips. The pirates settled back into place.

Minutes passed before Sugar returned.

"Any sign of Leo?" Christopher whispered with worry.

Sugar shook her head.

"I have to find him," Christopher said, rising. "Something's wrong. I know it. He should be here by now."

"Christopher," Lucy said calmly, "Leo told us to stay together. Give him a few more minutes."

"I can't."

Sugar pulled at his pant leg but before she or Lucy could do anything Christopher dashed from sight.

Frustrated, Lucy threw her hands into the air. "Great," she hissed while crossing her arms over her chest.

A third man approached the fire. "You boys need anything?"

Lucy's breath caught in her throat. "I know that voice," she gasped, peeking out from behind the rocks to confirm her suspicions. Mr. Bruce stood by the flames.

"Sugar, you have to get to him. If he sees you he'll

know we're here." Sugar nodded and as soon as Mr. Bruce walked away from the guards, she scrambled after him.

CHAPTER 62

Christopher made his way through the brambles toward the water. In the distance he heard Red Blade's hawk cry. Moonlight illuminated the bay. What had Leo told him about hawks? Leo's voice filled his head.

"Hawks are birds of prey. They feast on birds, bats, and small rodents."

Just then, halfway up the cliff side on a ledge above the water, Christopher spotted Leo.

His heart raced as he could see the hawk closing in.

*

"No use fighting me, rodent! I'll be dining on you one way or another!" The hawk laughed. Her talons gripped the jagged rocks and her neck bobbed toward Leo.

Leo reached between the crags for a long, sharp anemone quill that had been washed up by a storm. Leo raised it into the air like a sword.

"Not tonight!" he squeaked bravely.

The hawks eye's narrowed. "Don't make me laugh."

"En garde!"

The hawk flapped her wings, sending Leo against the rocks, but Leo kept his balance and quickly charged, piercing the hawk's broad chest with his quill.

"You will pay for that," the Hawk screamed. She plucked the quill from her chest with her bill.

The hawk closed the gap between them, her beak chomping down on the soft flesh of Leo's right ear. With a quick flip of her head, she threw the mouse into the air.

"Your choice mouse: die quickly by my beak or fall from the rocks and drown. Either way you'll be my breakfast."

Neither Leo nor the hawk heard Christopher approach.

"Never!" Leo quipped as Christopher pulled out his dagger and plunged the blade into the hawk's back.

With a cry the bird collapsed and Leo fell to his knees. "Your timing is impeccable," he squeaked breathlessly.

Christopher lay his hand down on the rock and smiled as he felt his friend's soft paws tickling his palm.

"Come on now," Christopher encouraged placing Leo upon his shoulder. "Let's not keep the girls waiting."

Christopher retrieved his knife and kicked the hawk's bloodied carcass into the swirling waters below.

CHAPTER 63

"Where did you go?" Lucy demanded when Christopher returned.

Christopher pulled his hair back from his shoulder exposing Leo. Blood dripped from the tiny mouse's ripped ear.

"Oh," she gasped, holding her hand to her chest. "Are you okay?"

Leo slicked back the tuft of matted fur covering his eyes and nodded. "I will be now," he squeaked.

A branch snapped to their left. Leo's one good ear stood on end.

"Christopher?" a man whispered. "Miss Lucy?" Mr. Bruce and Sugar stepped out of the shadows toward the children.

Lucy rushed toward the crusty sailor and flung her arms around his barrel chest. "Thank God you're alright."

"Where on earth did ye come from?" the surprised man asked.

"Cookie dropped us off in a bay just south of here before he sailed on to get help," Christopher replied. "Lucy spotted your campfire this afternoon."

Mr. Bruce exhaled. "When I saw Sugar, I didn't know what to think."

"Mr. Bruce," Lucy interrupted. "Is my father in that cave?"

"Aye, that he is. Officers too. Then there be the twins and Big John back on the Georgiana."

"I need to talk to my father."

"No, miss. It's too dangerous. The Captain would have my hide if he thought I put you in harm's way."

"Mr. Bruce, we need to do something. It might be too late by the time Cookie gets here with the Navy."

Reluctantly Mr. Bruce agreed. "I've been thinking the same thing all day. But there's no way to get the Captain and other officers out of the cave without being caught. Red Blade has too many men."

Lucy chewed her lower lip. "If Christopher and I can get my father out of the cave, do you think you can get us off of the island?"

"Aye . . . I think so. There is a smaller ship, a schooner called Revenge all but deserted out in the bay. It wouldn't take very many hands to sail her. We could probably even outrun the Dragon's Breath if we got enough of a head start."

Lucy's eyes sparkled as the corners of her mouth curled into a cautious smile.

"Then I think I have an idea."

Mr. Bruce shook his head. "Oh no you don't, young lady. Get them thoughts out of yer head."

"Christopher, can you get us into that cave so I can talk to my father tonight?"

When Christopher looked at Lucy, he noticed she was not looking at him but at the mouse, tucked behind his dirt-laden curls. Leo tugged on his ear. A bat circled in the night sky above their head.

"Yes," Christopher answered. "I can get you in."

CHAPTER 64

"While I was waiting for you," Lucy said, "I started to look around. That's when I discovered the lantana bushes."

Christopher and Mr. Bruce looked confused.

"These!" she said impatiently, pointing to several of the thickly dispersed flowering shrubs surrounding them. "The berries that are produced after the flower blooms are poisonous. If we gather the berries and grind them up we can put them in the pirates' drinking supplies. Whomever ingests the infected liquid will get violently ill. By the time the pirates figure out the source of their misfortune, it will be too late. We will already be gone."

Mr. Bruce cupped his chin. "I don't know, Miss Lucy. It sounds like an awful big risk."

Lucy huffed. "We used to have lantana shrubs all around our house in Antigua. They are not a nice plant. Papa was always worried that someone would accidentally eat the berries and get horribly ill. Our nanny, Miss Heffelfinger, used to warn us about the symptoms of the poisoning so we would know how to identify it if something happened. It takes several hours after the berries have been ingested before symptoms develop. If we put just a few ground berries into each bottle of rum and a handful of the paste into the water barrels, it will induce vomiting, fever, temporary blindness, and hallucinations. It's just what we need!

"Don't you see? If we infect their supplies tonight, when we return tomorrow, anyone who's had anything to drink during the day will be out cold."

Chapter 65

"Pesky creatures," Mr. Bruce said, swatting at a bat that flew too close for his liking. They were gathering the poisonous red berries in banana leaves while Lucy carefully pulverized them with a stick into a thick gooey paste. "You would think they like this stuff by the way they're hanging around."

"Ricardo!" Leo squeaked, rushing to his friend's aid in the rocks not far from where the others were gathering the berries.

"It's okay, mon. I be good. Just a close call with dat man's hand. Glad to see ju find da cave I told ju about."

"Yes, it's right where you said it would be," Leo stated. Ricardo brushed the sand from his wings.

"Ja, mon. Isabella's colony be liv'n in dar."

"My companions and I need to get into the cave. Do you think you could help us with the guards?"

"Is that what ju be call'n 'dem two nasty humans?"

Leo nodded. "Yes, and it is imperative that we send them away for a little bit so we can talk to our friends in the cave."

"It be me pleasure," Ricardo said, bobbing his head, his wide grin exposing two sharp front teeth. "Dis sounds like fun! I be want'n to do someding to dese grumpy humans, and from what I hear we be owing ju. Da rumor on da water be dat ju and dat boy be gotten rid of dat dang bothersome big bird dat be mak'n waves for us. Dat be true?"

"It is."

"Wow, mon! Ju and dat boy be one crack team. Dat bird be terrorizing us for years. Wait till I tell de odders. We all be jur friends forever. We help ju out any way ju want."

*

When an adequate amount of berries had been ground up, Lucy turned to Mr. Bruce.

"Mr. Bruce, are you sure you can get this into the supplies without us?" she asked.

"Aye, miss."

"Then I need to talk to my father."

Christopher bobbed his head in agreement. "You ready?" Leo had already told him the bats would create the diversion they needed.

"Let's go!"

"I don't like this," Mr. Bruce warned.

"Don't worry about us," Christopher told him. "Keep an eye on the guards and distract them if necessary. We'll be quick. I'll have Sugar come and find you when we're done."

Leo whistled for Ricardo.

Christopher and Lucy moved as close to the mouth of the cave as possible without being seen.

Seconds passed and the sky turned black as hundreds of bats flew out of the cave. The bats circled the guards' heads and dove at their faces.

"Shiver me timbers!" one shouted, waving an arm to protect himself.

The two men swatted and yelled, but the bats did not relent.

"What on earth?" Mr. Bruce gasped as the guards ran for cover.

"Now," Christopher whispered.

Before Mr. Bruce could hold them back, Christopher and Lucy slipped undetected into the cave.

Chapter 66

The shadows cast from the flames of the guards' fire danced across the damp rock walls.

"Papa," Lucy whispered tiptoeing toward the back of the cave.

The Captain and the other officers turned in the direction of Lucy's voice.

"Lucy?" he questioned. "Darling, is that you?"

"Yes, Papa," she answered, running towards him.

The Captain and the officers hung from a net tied to the ceiling of the cave. They were tired and bruised but in good health overall. Christopher feared that the Captain would be angry with him for coming to find them, but he wasn't; he was just relieved to see Lucy.

"Christopher," the Captain said, squeezing his arm affectionately. "What are you doing here?"

"Sir, I'd really like to explain everything, but we don't have much time."

"Where's Cookie?" the Captain asked, panic in his voice.

"He sailed on to get help, as you instructed. He didn't know the island he dropped us on was the same island where the pirates made camp. He thought it was deserted."

"Papa," Lucy interrupted, "we've got a plan to get you out of here."

Lucy told him about the berries and how at this very minute Mr. Bruce was tainting the pirates' supplies.

"Children," Mr. Miller said, "be careful with your dosages. We don't want to give the pirates too much. Let the Royal Navy deliver the punishments, not you."

Lucy nodded. "Yes, sir. We'll be back tomorrow night," she said as they turned to leave. "And remember: don't drink anything they give you."

"Be careful!" the Captain advised.

Chapter 67

As the sun began to rise, the four friends tucked in under the shade of their sleeping platform and fell asleep.

Christopher, the first to wake, stretched. His body ached and his hands, still bruised, throbbed. He made fists then released them to see if he could get the blood flowing again. A swim would soothe them, he thought. Sugar still slept soundly curled in Lucy's arms, and even Leo snored softly on his bed of leaves.

Christopher crawled out from under their shelter as quietly as possible and headed toward the water. He couldn't shake the feeling that something was still amiss. The pirates' drinks were all tainted, but he didn't know if that would be enough to guarantee their escape.

Several groups of red-breasted bullfinches sang out from the trees above. Their calls were playful, nothing like the shrill screams of the hawk the night before.

Christopher walked the beach along the treeline until he reached the towering high sandstone cliff to the left of their camp. Then he headed toward the water, letting the waves cool his feet. He hoped there were some very thirsty pirates two bays down from where he stood.

Christopher walked back up to the beach and sat quietly underneath a lone breadfruit tree.

"Ow," he said, picking at the thorny vine lodged in his back. He dug around in the sand to see if there were any more surprises and pulled out three other creepers buried around the base of the tree. He tried to brush the vines aside but their small thorns stuck to his hand. The more he touched the vines, the more entangled he became.

"That hurts," he moaned, dislodging the thorns with the help of a branch. He rubbed the spots where the vines had clung to his skin.

"That's it!" he exclaimed to himself. Lucy had come up with the berries plan; why hadn't he thought of this? Everywhere Christopher looked there was something they could use against the pirates. He slapped his forehead and shook his head. Lesson One. Know your surroundings. Leo was right, you cannot pick the time in which you truly learn something. It just happens.

Christopher picked his way over to a large cactus. What was it he had read about these? The sap from the candelabra cactus causes burning blisters. If it gets into the eyes it can cause temporary blindness lasting several hours.

When he turned around, he discovered that the rocky hillside was covered in sisal plants. He remembered reading that sap from a cut sisal leaf produces immediate burning, itching, and swelling.

Christopher couldn't believe his eyes. This was just what he had been looking for. They already tainted the pirates' drinking supplies, so now it was time to sabotage the rest of their camp.

Chapter 68

Christopher laid out his plant samples on the sand. "Wake up!"

"What time is it?" Leo moaned and yawned, scratching the top of his head.

Christopher shrugged. "I don't know."

Leo circled Christopher's makeshift display. "Hmm," he mumbled, looking over the various plants Christopher had gathered. "Where did you get these?"

"Just down at the end of the beach."

Leo picked up a vine. The thorns wrapped his paw. "That's not nice!"

Sugar screeched and came to help.

"Exactly! It's awful. The same thing happened to me, which got me thinking . . ."

"What's that?" Lucy asked pointing to the cactus with one hand and rubbing her eyes with the other.

"Our secondary defense," Christopher said. "I've been thinking about the lantana berries all morning. What if that isn't enough? We need to be able to slow the pirates down so they can't come after us right away. Remember how Mr. Bruce said he thought the schooner could outrun the larger warship if given enough time? Well this is how we get the time."

Leo circled the pile. "He's right."

"If we spread the sap along the gunwales and over the oars, whomever touches them will be affected—blisters, rashes, swelling, blindness, everything. Red Blade can't sail the Dragon's Breath by himself. Instead, he'll be stuck on the island until his crew has recovered. Then, we can bury the vines just under the sand. Anyone who walks on them will get completely tangled up. It happened to me just now as I sat on the beach, just like you, Leo."

Lucy clapped. "Brilliant!"

As evening approached, they carefully wrapped the thorny vines in giant banana leaves and filled empty shells with the irritating saps. All that was left to do was wait.

Chapter 69

The pirate camp was deathly quiet as they approached.

"Do you think the berries worked?" Lucy whispered.

Christopher shrugged.

"Sugar and I will go have a look. You two make your way to the beach and take care of the dories."

Lucy stopped walking. "Careful," Christopher said bumping into her.

"Did you hear that?"she asked.

"I think it came from over there." Christopher pointed toward a grove of palm trees.

Lucy shivered despite the heat. "Where do you think everyone is?"

Leo darted across the path in front of them. "There are two men farther down the beach," he panted. "Beyond the boats, but they're pretty sick. The rest of the camp seems to have had plenty to drink too. The berries worked just like you said."

Lucy grinned, and Leo continued.

"Sugar is counting the sailors to make sure we have a proper head count. We will meet you at the cave."

Christopher nodded. The moon disappeared behind a passing cloud and the rough trail they followed was cast in shadows. "Watch your step."

"There," Lucy pointed tapping Christopher's shoulder. Five boats sat in the sand. The cloud passed.

"Leave the last one untouched," Christopher said. "We'll use that one to get out to the schooner."

Lucy nodded and began to pour sap from the shell in her hand onto the oarlocks.

A branch snapped and a pirate with a red sash tied around his head crashed through the shrubbery, tripping on a root.

"Don't move." Christopher said, pulling Lucy to his side behind the transom of the first boat.

Inches from the dory, the man dropped to his knees and then landed with a thud face down in the sand in front of them.

"Ew," Lucy gagged, turning into Christopher's shoulder. "Tell me that's not vomit on his shirt."

Christopher winced and turned away from the man. "I can't." He turned back to the unconscious man and nudged him with his toe. When he didn't move, they went back to work.

CHAPTER 70

Leo scurried toward them as they approached the cave.

"Where are the guards?" Lucy asked.

"Over there." Leo pointed to the two still forms lying in the sand on the far side of the cave's entrance. "Sugar's gone to find Mr. Bruce."

A light breeze blew across the bay and danced through the trees, rustling the palm fronds.

"Lucy? Christopher?" Mr. Bruce said walking into the clearing with Sugar right behind him swinging through the low branches.

"We're here," Christopher replied, placing Leo in the pouch.

Mr. Bruce sighed and then took a deep breath, relieved to find the children safe.

"Shall we?" Lucy asked impatiently, thinking of her father and of getting as far away from the island as possible.

"Aye, miss," Mr. Bruce concurred, picking up the torch propped up against the mouth of the cave and dipping it into the fire.

"Follow me."

The officers turned as the chamber filled with light.

"Lucy?" the Captain whispered.

"Papa!"

Mr. Bruce rushed to the net. "Hurry, children."

Christopher eased the line allowing the men to break free.

"Where's Mr. Miller?" Christopher asked seeing he was not with the other officers.

"They took him out at midday to help with the men who were getting sick," Mr. Johnson replied, rubbing the red welts the ropes had left on his arms. "He had no choice; they had a cutlass to his back."

"Let's move," the Admiral said, patting Christopher on the shoulder. "There's nothing we can do for Mr. Miller. He's a valued commodity in this kind of community. He'll be safe for now."

But as they made their way out of the cave, Christopher thought about how not having Mr. Miller would hurt their chances of escaping. They needed everyone in order to sail the schooner from the bay, and Mr. Miller was bigger and a seasoned sailor, stronger than most. Christopher knew his size would have made a considerable difference.

Once outside the cave, from the path leading to the water Christopher saw a lantern burning in the cook shack.

"I know where he is," Christopher whispered to Mr. Bruce, pointing to the light.

"Aye," the older man agreed.

"We need him."

Mr. Bruce grimaced. "I fear you're right, but we've no time to spare."

"I'll be quick!"Christopher said as he took off toward the shack with Sugar chattering softly while pulling at his pant leg. "Let's go get him, girl."

Chapter 71

Christopher's heart rate doubled as he approached Mr. Miller, who was poking at a man lying on the table.

"Arrgh, ye best be fix'n me mate here, or it'll be lead ye be tastin'," another man said, aiming a shaky pistol at the doctor. His voice was thick and his speech slurred with the effects of the poison he'd ingested as well.

"Pointing that at me will not help your friend," said Dr. Miller as he continued working.

A single lantern burned from the rafters above them. The man with the pistol sat on a stool, his upper body leaning back against the wall, out of Christopher's sight except for the light reflecting off his shiny black boots.

Christopher drew in a deep breath, realizing what those boots meant.

"What is it?" Leo said peeking from his pouch.

Christopher couldn't speak.

Focusing on the men in the room, Leo understood. "Oh dear." He scampered to the ground.

Boots lurched forward, turning toward the door. "Who be there?" he yelled into the darkness. He wiped the sweat from his brow and staggered forward, grabbing the nearby post to steady himself.

"You really should stay seated," Mr. Miller told him, motioning at the stool.

"Don't ye be tell'n me what to do, you worthless piece of whale blubber!"

"You do not look well, and yelling is definitely not helping you or your friend."

Christopher didn't move; he couldn't. His legs refused to work. Seeing Boots again left him paralyzed with fear, but it was too late to turn back. He would look foolish for leaving the group if he didn't return with Mr. Miller. Forcing himself, he crawled closer.

Boots swayed on his way back to his stool but before he reached it, he turned around and shouted out the door, "I said, who be there?"

Christopher should have guessed he would be too stubborn to give in to the poison. He threw three large rocks into the brush on the other side of the clearing. Boots cursed then staggered in the direction of the sounds.

"Mr. Miller," Christopher whispered. Branches cracked, and a thud hinted that Boots had fallen. "Mr. Miller!" Christopher whispered more loudly.

"Christopher! What in the . . . ?"

"Quick! Follow me!"

Christopher hustled the doctor out of the cook shack,

pushing the doctor along in front of him. He was breathing hard. "Over there. The dory! Hurry!"

Mr. Miller nodded. "I see them."

Christopher slowed and finally stopped, looking for Leo and whistled to Sugar, who had disappeared into the brush. Mr. Miller continued on.

"Ha!" Boots slurred, leaping in front of the boy. The pirate squinted through his one good eye. "I be wonder'n where ye been."

Mr. Miller, already at the beach, was too far ahead to see Boots lift Christopher into the air and throw him into the trunk of a palm tree. The air whooshed from Christopher's lungs, and he landed with a thud in the sand.

Chapter 72

"Where's Christopher?" the Captain asked as Mr. Miller splashed toward the dory just outside of the breaking waves.

"He was right behind me!" he said, looking back toward the shore.

"I'll get him," Mr. Bruce huffed, jumping from the boat.

"No!" the Admiral ordered, standing in the bow. "He's a smart boy. He will be fine, but if we don't leave now we are all doomed. As soon as we get reinforcements we'll come back for him. You have my word."

Lucy grasped the rail. "You can't be serious! He just saved your lives. We can't leave him!"

The Captain placed his hand on his daughter's shoulder, holding her in place. "Get back in the boat, Mr. Bruce." He ordered, bowing his head. "The Admiral is right. There is no time."

CHAPTER 73

A sudden burst of wind blew Christopher's hair from his face. The drumming beat of thousands of wings flooded his ears. The sky turned black as a cloud of bats descended on Boots, their razor sharp talons drawn. Boots' lanky form disappeared. The bats swooped at his face and shredded his clothing. The pirate screamed and cursed, covering his head with his arms.

"Follow me!" Leo yelled to Christopher from Sugar's back as they galloped toward the swarm of angry bats. Christopher pushed to his feet and ran toward the monkey.

Boots broke free of the swarm, swinging his arms in the air.

"Quickly!" Leo urged.

Boots staggered toward them as the bats continued diving at his head.

"This way!" Leo screamed.

Sugar changed directions and darted toward the dense brush behind the camp.

"Get back here, boy!" Boots yelled.

The bats circled his head blurring Christopher from

sight. Loose rock crumbled beneath his feet. The boy was getting away.

"Arrgh!!!!" he screamed as his foot snagged a branch.

Christopher heard Boots fall.

"Follow me!" Ricardo called, breaking from his colony and weaving through the trees toward the far cliffs that surrounded the bay.

"Where are we going?" Christopher gasped.

"Ricardo knows a place where you can hide!" Leo yelled.

"But Lucy?"

"They already left."

"What?" Christopher's heart sank.

"They had to, Christopher, but they'll be back. Lucy would never abandon you."

"What about our camp?"

"It's too open. We can't risk returning to it until the pirates leave."

Chapter 74

Running as fast as they could they followed Ricardo to the base of the bluff.

"Dis way!" he screeched, darting along the jagged rocks along the water's edge. "Around de point."

"Hurry!" Leo chanted.

The surf crashed around Christopher, wetting his feet, while Leo and Sugar leapt across the smaller rock overhangs jutting out above him.

As they rounded the corner, Ricardo flew into a narrow gap formed by wind and surge.

"We're here, mon. Dis be de best cave on all de island."

Christopher glared at the opening. "I can't fit in there!"

"Yes you can!" Leo shouted. "It will be tight, but you can make it." Waves crashed around him covering him in spray. Christopher looked to the ledge thirty feet above wondering if there was another way in. Sugar screeched.

Christopher inhaled deeply. Salt water surged around him. Timing his entrance with the lulls he counted, one, two, three. The back of his shirt snagged on a rock and ripped as he struggled to slip sideways through the gap.

"I told you you'd fit," Leo said.

Once inside, the cave opened up and the water around his feet became stilled. On the other side of the large luminous pool was a smooth, dry rock platform tucked under a tall, arching overhang. Above that, a series of smaller tunnels were etched into the mountainside.

"Over here!" Leo waved his paws in the air.

Christopher waded into the clear, undisturbed light blue water and looked into the endless dark caverns above his head.

"This whole bluff is hollow," Leo squeaked. "Ricardo said his family had lived in here for hundreds of years . . . until Captain Red Blade and his men arrived."

"Ju like?" Ricardo asked Leo happily.

"It's perfect. Thank you."

"Good! Den I leave ju for a little while and check in on me mates. I be back dough."

CHAPTER 75

Christopher shivered next to Sugar on the dry rocks under the ledge.

Leo yawned.

Cluck, shhh, clunk, shhh, clunk.

"What's that?' Christopher whispered.

Leo's ears perked.

"Cap'n?" boomed a raspy voice startling the small mouse.

Sugar cringed. Torchlight bounced off the rock walls above their heads forcing them further beneath the ledge and into the shadows.

"Cap'n?

"What?" the cave walls vibrated.

Leo's tiny eyes bulged. Christopher put his finger to his lips.

Cluck, shhh, clunk, shhh, clunk.

The uneven footsteps faded and the light dimmed. Leo crawled out from where they had been crouched.

"Cap'n?" the man called a third time as he reached a "T" in the tunnel.

"Here!" came a growl.

Leo leapt from ledge to ledge until he reached the mouth of the upper cave where the sailor had been; Christopher and Sugar followed in close pursuit.

"Stay here," Leo warned, herding his friends behind a darkened corner to which the pirate had not turned. "I'll be right back."

A bright light shone from an opened door at the end of the corridor.

Cluck, shhh, clunk, shhh, clunk.

CHAPTER 76

"What?" Red Blade snarled as the sailor limped forward on a pegged leg.

Leo scurried through the tunnel toward the voices.

Red Blade pushed back from his desk. "I told ye never to bother me whilst in my lair!" he said, pounding his fist down upon the table. The candles flickered.

The crewman quivered.

"Pardon me, Cap'n, but…"

"No buts!" Red Blade's coal-colored eyes narrowed.

Leo scurried behind an open trunk of gold and jewels.

The sickly crewman wobbled on his worn wooden leg.

"Someth'n happened down at the camp." The sailor steadied himself against the edge of the table. He himself had been unconscious until Boots stumbled into the center of camp screaming about bats and a missing boy.

"Sir, it's Boots. He's gone mad. The crew doesn't know what to do with him and . . ."

Red Blade raised his hand in the air silencing his crewman before he could finish. He had been in the cave for over a day. He fingered a pile of doubloons, dropping several to the floor, "If ye doubt his sanity, feed him to the sharks."

"But, sir, it's more than just Boots. The whole crew be get'n sick. There be not one solid man in camp whose belly and head ain't been to see the devil. There be no way any of us could even manage a kill'n in the shape we be in." The sailor's shoulders slumped; he was having a hard time staying upright. His only knee quivered.

Red Blade fingered the jeweled handle of a prince's dagger he had stolen. "And the prisoners?"

The crewman shook his head. "Gone. Along with the Revenge."

Chapter 77

Red Blade fired his pistol into the air, reloaded it, brought back the pin, and fired a second shot between the two sleeping men outside of the cave.

"Wake up you useless scallywags!" he roared. The guards struggled to their feet. "The Devil take you," Red Blade cursed and looked to the sky as he began to reload. The brightening blue above alerted him of the time. The prisoners had escaped, but they couldn't have gone far.

Red Blade stormed to the center of camp. "What is this?" he bellowed, kicking one of his crew. The sailor flinched but did not move.

"Rise and gather! The prisoners have escaped!"

Red Blade fired a third shot at the water barrel as he approached the open cook's shack. He let the water run out into his cupped hand and held it up to his nose.

"Poison!" he boomed, grabbing an empty rum bottle and smelling its tainted remnants as well.

Boots trembled as he approached, the poisons still pulsing through his weakened body. His head throbbed. Stinky, now conscious, had done his best to help clean him up but blood still trickled down the side of his head from where he'd fallen after chasing the boy. The useless piece of whale dung had to be somewhere near by.

Red Blade scowled. "Gather the men and head out to the Dragon's Breath. I want the prisoners and the Revenge in my sights by noon!" he ordered, deciding not to waste any more ammunition on Boots.

"Aye," Boots moaned, wobbling toward the bay.

"Arrgh," his brethren replied.

Chapter 78

Leo hurried back to his friends as soon as he saw that Red Blade had stormed into camp.

"Follow me," he squeaked excitedly, leading them up the ledge and toward Red Blade's treasure hold. "In here." Christopher opened the door. The candles flickered.

Gold and silver coins spilled onto the floor from inside sea chests. Piles of precious jewels flowed over into glorious, glowing mounds. Christopher gasped. The piles of stolen goods climbed to the ceiling. He walked to Red Blade's desk and fingered a dagger stuck into its thick lacquered surface. Rubies lined the handle's belly and a sapphire bigger than his eye crowned the pommel. With a single pull he freed it. Not in his wildest dreams could he have imagined what lay in front of him.

"All this is Red Blade's?"

Christopher could not fathom the amount of blood that must have been shed to amass such a treasure.

Leo climbed up the leg of the desk wearing a ring made of rubies and diamonds as a crown. "Yes, I believe so."

"And he knows about the Captain's escape?"

"Yes, I heard him order his men to ready the boats."

Christopher hoped that the schooner was well out of harm's way.

Sugar chattered excitedly from atop a pile of jewels with an elaborate bracelet of emeralds around her neck.

"Well then," Christopher said as he shoved the dagger into his belt and placed Leo on his shoulder. "Let's make sure he's found the other presents we left."

Christopher grabbed several candles from the silver candelabra on the desk and blew out all but one.

"This way," Leo said.

Christopher nodded. "Lead the way, human guide."

As he shut the door behind them, he decided that if he got out of this mess alive, he would bring Lucy back here and let her pick out whatever she liked.

CHAPTER 79

Lucy leaned against the rail of the small schooner feeling unsettled. She chewed her lip and thought about Christopher.

"Jibe ho!" came the call from the back of the schooner. The heavy single wooden boom of the larger aft mast groaned as it crossed the deck. Mr. Bruce had been right: the Revenge was fast under sail and small enough to handle with only a few strong men.

Lucy glanced back at Mr. Johnson standing at the helm. She didn't feel like being social. She watched as the waves crested and disappeared in a never-ending cycle.

"Lucy, darling," the Captain said, approaching her. He placed his hands on her shoulders. He intended to comfort her, but as she had not heard him approach, instead she jumped at his touch.

"Sorry, I didn't mean to startle you."

Lucy leaned into her father.

"When did you say Cookie left you?"

"Three days ago, Papa."

"Hmm," the Captain said, stepping back to scratch at

the graying stubble on his chin. He was not used to facial hair and found it extremely uncomfortable. "You look worried, darling."

"I am."

"Please don't be. I'm not sure what happened to Christopher, but I have confidence that he will be alright. We shall see him again very soon."

Lucy's head dipped. "How long until we make port?"

"It is not far. If we are lucky we will be there before supper."

Mr. Bruce stood on the bow keeping watch on the horizon. They expected the pirates to have discovered their absence by now.

"Papa, do you think the pirates are coming after us already?"

"Yes. It has been several hours. We would be foolish to think they are not. But we have had a good head start and with any luck we will reach Tortola before them."

CHAPTER 80

Leo led his friends through the maze of tunnels to the main entrance. From there they could hear the shouts of the men below as they cleared the beach and made ready to sail. Christopher lay in the wild grass next to the cave's entrance and extended his spyglass to watch.

"Avast ye scurvy dogs! Get to the boats!" Red Blade shouted.

"Me eyes!" a man yelled, leaping into the water.

"Blast be these cursed vines!" screamed another.

"Do you think we've delayed them long enough?" Christopher asked as Red Blade's crew finally managed to row to the Dragon's Breath.

The mouse shrugged. "I'm not sure, but by my calculations the Captain should have a good four-hour lead."

Christopher puffed the hair from his eyes.

"Dere ju be, mon," Ricardo called, landing next to Leo. "Dem be a sorry lot of man creatures down dere. I never be hear'n so much moan'n and groan'n in all me life." The bat clutched his belly and laughed. "Nobody be left in camp now. De whole place be empty as can be. I left half me colony down dere just in case. Dey tell ju if I be wrong, but I be pretty sure all dem sorry humans get on dat dare big ol' red float'n island."

Only the merchant vessel remained in the bay. The afternoon sun warmed Christopher's back, making him yawn.

"Why don't you get some rest?" Leo suggested.

Christopher collapsed the spyglass and put it back in his pocket. Then he leaned against a tree and promptly fell asleep.

CHAPTER 81

"Ship to starboard!"

Lucy strained to see the shadow off the port side rail. Mr. Johnson said they were only a couple hours from Tortola. Could that be someone sailing from the harbor now, or was it something else all together?

"Give me a glass!" the Admiral shouted.

Lucy's father took the wheel. "What's her course?"

"She's heading straight for us, Captain!" Mr. Johnson replied.

"Lighten the boat. We need more speed!"

CHAPTER 82

As the sun set, Christopher's stomach growled.

Leo's ear perked up. "Shall we see what the pirates left behind?"

A brilliant full moon lit the lifeless camp. The charred bits of what had been the cook's fire smoldered in the corner. Christopher examined the shattered remains of the water barrel.

"I guess they figured out that we tainted the supplies," he said, continuing to look for food.

"Over here," Leo squeaked, standing in front of several sealed barrels that lay hidden behind a grouping of banana trees.

Christopher rolled a barrel over to the clearing and pried open the top. The familiar aroma of pickled fish invaded his nose and he gagged. "You must be kidding!" He shuddered and bagged the top back in place.

"This should do," Leo squeaked, finding a canvas bag stuffed with spiced dried meats. Sugar screeched and rolled a wax-sealed wheel of cheese in their direction.

Christopher looked out into the bay. A lantern burned

in Captain Hughes' old stateroom on the Georgiana.

"Someone is still out there," Christopher said, swallowing a chunk of dried jerk pork.

Leo whistled to Ricardo, who had remained close-by giving them updates through out the day.

"Ja, mon?"

"Will you to see who's out there?" Leo asked.

Ricardo flew toward the bobbing galleon. Christopher cut the cheese into chunks with Red Blade's dagger and walked toward the beach.

"It be like dis," Ricardo told Leo when he returned. "Dare be tree men down in de bottom of de human island behind big metal bars and one man walk'n free."

Leo's whiskers twitched. "The twins and Big John are still here."

"What happens to them if Red Blade returns before the Navy?" Christopher asked, afraid of the answer.

"It will probably depend on whether or not he caught up to the Captain. "

"How many guards?" Leo asked Ricardo.

"Just one."

Christopher smiled. "Let's go get them."

CHAPTER 83

The beach had been swept clean and the vines removed—but the dories were gone, too. Christopher looked across the empty white sand and wondered how to get out to the Georgiana.

"There," Leo said, spotting a small rowboat tied to the side of the ship. "Do you see that?"

Ricardo swooped down and landed on Christopher's outstretched hand, joining them at the water's edge.

"Yes, but how are we get it? Reef sharks feed at night and I don't really feel like being someone's dinner."

Ricardo chirped.

"What did he say?" Christopher asked.

"Just wait," Leo said smiling.

Ricardo flapped his wings several times as he circled their heads. Soon more bats joined him, forming a pulsing black cloud.

"Watch this," Leo said, his black eyes shining.

The bats flew to the Georgiana.

"Leo?"

"Wait . . ." the little mouse beamed and held his palm

in the air.

The bats surrounded the rowboat.

"Chew da line," Ricardo instructed the swarm.

The thick twine holding the rowboat snapped. The bats circled the boat and grabbed its top rail with their razor sharp claws.

On Ricardo's command the bats flapped their wings and the dory moved into the bay.

When the boat was close enough to shore, Christopher waded out, grabbed the bow, and the bats dispersed.

"Well done," Christopher said, holding his hand out to help Sugar and Leo aboard. After placing the oars in their locks, he rowed silently to the Georgiana.

The aft port lights illuminated a man sitting in the Captain's cabin with his feet resting on top of his table.

"To Neptune!" he yelled, raising a bottle high. The lantern light reflected off his newly shaven head.

A chill ran down Christopher's spine as the man turned and the bulging shirtless warrior glared out the window. Luckily, the Georgiana's shadow hid them from sight, though.

The pirate started to sing and Sugar covered her ears.

"I know, girl." Christopher empathized, wishing he could do the same.

CHAPTER 84

"Tie up here," Leo instructed halfway down the leeward side. "I'll be right back."

Leo bolted up the outer rail and darted down the empty deck noticing that the door to the Captain's cabin where Red Blade's guard remained was closed. After scampering down the forward hatch Leo reached the lower levels where the loyal crewmen were kept. Leo scanned the room for sign of a key and spotted it hanging on a peg just outside the door.

"Okay," he said upon his return to Christopher. "The deck is clear and the key to the brig is on the wall." Leo lowered a rope down to Christopher so he could climb aboard.

"Sugar, be our lookout," Christopher said, putting her down. Sugar's head bobbed as she climbed up the ratlines to the first mid-mast platform. "Let's go."

"There," Leo pointed from Christopher's shoulder.

The men behind the iron bars turned.

"Who's there?" Big John called out. Nathan and Henry crowded the bars.

"It's me," Christopher whispered while peeking through the door. Three sets of wide eyes stared back.

"You speak?" Henry asked Christopher.

"Yes."

Nathan clutched the bars, his knuckles turning white. "You're not one of them, are you?"

Christopher slid the key for the peg. "No." The lock clicked.

"What are you doing here, Christopher?" Big John asked.

"It's a long story that I'll happily tell you once we are safe," Christopher replied.

"I will hold you to that."

Nathan picked up a wooden stay. "Where's the guard?"

"He's singing in the Captain's cabin."

Henry rolled his eyes. "I think that's how Red Blade intended to torture us."

Nathan hit Henry on the shoulder.

"What?" His brother gasped, throwing his hands in the air. "You know the man can't carry a tune."

Big John stilled. "Come now lads; quit your bickering."

"We should do something with the guard or he'll come looking for us as soon as we're free," Christopher said.

"Aye," Big John agreed.

Christopher thought for a moment. "If I can get him out of the cabin, do you think you three can take him down?" Henry, Nathan, and Big John nodded.

"Okay." Christopher looked at Sugar. "Think you can distract him, girl?"

"Eep!" Sugar answered.

Christopher reached for Leo when no one was looking and placed him on to the deck next to her. "Try and get him to chase you, Leo. I'll be waiting by the door. When I hear you coming, I'll open it and you run for the dory."

Chapter 85

Leo entered Lucy's cabin through a hole at the base of her built-in bunk and squeezed beneath the door into the main salon. Being small had its advantages.

The pirate guard sat in a dining chair, the Captain's empty silver goblet at his side and a half-eaten tray of rotting food on the table in front of him.

From the other side of the open stern light Leo spotted Sugar. She hung from a line cast from the outer rail dangling in the air just beyond the cabin. With a nod from Leo, she crawled through.

"What be this?" the pirate gasped. Sugar bared her teeth. The pirate pushed to his feet and Leo dashed up the man's loose pant leg and bit the skin directly behind his knee. The guard screamed and hopped from one foot to the other. Sugar leapt from the window ledge, landed on the pirate's back, and started pulling at his ears.

From outside Christopher heard the clatter of furniture breaking and opened the door. Leo and Sugar sprinted through followed closely by the pirate who stumbled onto the deck.

"Take that!" Nathan yelled, brandishing the long wooden baton he'd grabbed to use as a weapon. With a yell he raised his makeshift sword while Henry swung from a halyard. The guard reached for his saber only to remember that he had left it inside. Henry's feet caught the man in the chest and pushed him into the wall. Nathan struck his belly with a thud and Big John brought an iron block down upon his head. The guard crumbled to the ground.

"Tie him up lads," Big John said, wiping his hands clean on his shirttails. "Give him food and water for a couple of days and leave him in the brig as he done to us."

CHAPTER 86

Christopher watched as the four men slept peacefully on the platform he and Lucy had constructed days earlier. Not a breath of wind touched the bay, and even the leaves above his head refused to move. Too hot to sleep, Christopher sighed.

"Come on," Leo said, leading Christopher to the water. "Let's see what we can catch for supper." Christopher took off his shirt and dropped it in the sand above the high tide line.

The water welcomed him in its cool embrace as he dove underneath its velvety surface repeatedly. As he emerged from his third dive, he looked back at the beach. Leo was jumping up and down, waving him in.

"What?" Christopher said, hitting the side of his head with his hand to get the water out of his ears.

"Ship!" Leo squeaked as the bow pulpit of a large sailing vessel drifted around the point. Christopher grabbed his shirt and sprinted back to the camp.

After seizing his spyglass and the pirate guard's pistol from the night before, Christopher quickly shook his companions awake.

"A ship," he panted. "I'm going to the point to see who it is. Stay out of sight!"

Christopher bound up the hill to the top of the bluff, his heart skipping a beat with every glimpse of the sturdy wooden prow.

Ducking behind a boulder he extended the spyglass.

"It's them!" he shouted to Leo and Sugar as they came sprinting up behind him. Christopher collapsed the spyglass while running to the cliff's edge.

There, sailing through the channel, was the Revenge skippered by Captain Hughes and being escorted by two British frigates. The Admiral, now in command, stood proudly at the stern of the warship in the lead.

"Here!" Christopher yelled. He pulled the pistol from his pants and fired a shot into the air. The sailors on the frigates rushed to ready their muskets.

"There!" Cookie yelled, from the deck of the Revenge as he spotted Christopher on the cliff.

"Stand down!" the Admiral ordered.

Lucy raced to the rail. "Christopher!"

Christopher could hear the sheets ease as the Revenge changed course. He darted along the edge of the rocks calling to Big John and the others.

The Royal Navy's frigates continued toward the pirate's safe harbor, but the Revenge tacked and changed course to their bay.

Christopher heard a dory splash down as he made it to the beach and watched excitedly as Mr. Bruce rowed Lucy, Cookie, and the Captain ashore.

As they neared the beach Lucy jumped into the water and ran to Christopher.

"You're okay!" she shouted and hugged him.

"Yes," he beamed. He could feel her breath on his cheek as she whispered how sorry she was that they had left him behind.

"It's alright," he whispered. "I was never alone."

Lucy smiled, burying her face in his neck. "I know."

The Captain cleared his throat, "Ahem . . ." Christopher blushed and begrudgingly released his daughter.

"Sir," he said, bowing his head.

Cookie chuckled then pulled Christopher into his chest for a hug.

Christopher soon learned that after setting sail, the Captain and his crew met up with Cookie, who had reached the Royal Navy the day before. While the Admiral was telling his fellow officers what had happened, Captain Red Blade and the Dragon's Breath came into view. The Dragon's Breath was no match for the four naval frigates coming to find them and was soon overpowered. Two of the frigates were now escorting her back to Tortola.

Lucy stood at Christopher's side as her father told the story. "I'll never desert you like that again. If I had known you weren't behind Mr. Miller, I would never have gotten in the dory. What on earth happened to you? Where did you go?"

"Boots found me."

"Oh no!"

"It's okay. I had some help."

Lucy smiled. "I bet you did."

Cookie cocked his head.

Christopher pulled the jeweled dagger from his pants. "Captain?"

Cookie's eyes grew wide.

"There's something else I need to show you."

Chapter 87

The Captain, Lucy, Cookie, and Sugar followed Christopher down the dirt path toward Red Blade's cave.

When they reached the entrance, Christopher passed them each a half-burnt candle from the candelabra he had stashed in the shrubs earlier.

"Well blow me down," Cookie gulped, looking around the treasure chamber. A fortune of gold and jewels sparkled in the torchlight.

Silently, the Captain walked through the room taking in the sheer abundance of wealth that lay before him.

"This treasure is not ours," he said at last. "It has been stolen and needs to be returned."

Lucy squeezed Christopher's arm as she caressed the enormous strand of pearls he had just placed over her head.

"I am sure that the owners of many of these items will eagerly offer a fair reward to whomever is responsible for finding them. After that, maritime law states that whatever treasure is left unclaimed belongs to the person who found it. "

Lucy looked at Christopher. "That's you," she told him. "You're going to be rich."

"Eep!" said Sugar as she frolicked in a pile of gold coins.

Christopher stared out at the treasure in shock. He had never thought, not even for a moment, that any of this would be his someday.

"No more worries for you, young man," Cookie said joyfully, slapping him on the back. A crown fit for a king teetered upon his hairless head.

"He's right, son," the Captain declared. "You are a free and wealthy man now, or at least you will be soon between your rewards and whatever remains unclaimed."

Christopher looked at Lucy and the Captain and then at Cookie and Sugar. He knew that all that really mattered was standing right in front of him or, in the case of his human guide, resting peacefully in his side pouch. For the first time since losing his parents, Christopher felt truly happy.

CHAPTER 88

The trip to Tortola on the Georgiana went quickly. As soon as they reached port the Captain sent news of their return to his wife.

Cookie told the Navy where he had hidden the ammunition and they happily assisted the Captain in handling the remaining technicalities regarding his ship's original cargo.

The treasure was unloaded, sorted, and catalogued, and the Admiral personally assured Christopher that he would see to the details himself.

"What of the pirates?" Christopher asked.

"Red Blade and his crew have already been tried. They will hang for their crimes."

"And Boots?"

The Admiral shook his head. "I was informed that he went crazy on the way to Tortola. My men told me he screamed of devil bats before leaping from the ship."

"I see," Christopher said, making eye contact with Lucy.

"Christopher, my offer still stands," said the Admiral. "If it is a life at sea you wish, I can promise you that His

Majesty's Royal Navy would welcome you with open arms. I would even insist on overseeing your first placement."

"Thank you, sir," Christopher replied humbly. "May I have some time to think about it?"

"Take all the time you need, young man. As long as I am in the Navy, my offer will remain open."

The Captain cleared his throat. "I have been thinking of your future as well, Christopher. While you take the time to ponder the Admiral's kind offer, I would ask you to consider joining Lucy and me in Antigua. If you find you like it there, I would be honored if you would consider becoming a permanent part of our family."

Christopher could not speak. He thought of the uncle he never met in London and of his parents' sudden deaths.

"Take a couple of days to weigh your options. You can let me know when you are ready."

Christopher swallowed hard. "Thank you, sir."

CHAPTER 89

The warm Caribbean trade winds gently carried the Georgiana home to Antigua. Christopher's last two days at sea were blissful and merry.

On the morning they sailed into the English Harbor, church bells rang out and the Captain and his loyal crew members were hailed as heroes. Everyone, it seemed, turned out to welcome them. Apparently the Captain's letters to his wife had reached their destination and spread the news before their arrival.

As the ship tied up to the bulkhead, Christopher looked down from the guardrails at the crowd below.

"Tuck your shirt in," Leo instructed. "And stand up straight."

"Come on, Christopher," Lucy urged. Christopher's palms started to sweat.

"Are you coming?" he asked Leo.

"I will meet you there. I promised Sugar I would help her organize the galley, and she said she would bring me up to the plantation this evening. Go on now," Leo prodded, seeing that Lucy would not be satisfied until

Christopher followed her. "It's better you're on your own anyway. You wouldn't want the missus to think you kept company with a mouse, now would you?" Leo's black eyes smiled up at him giving Christopher the courage to fall in step with Lucy.

"I can see my mum. She's right over there. Don't worry, Christopher. She'll love you. And there are my sisters." Lucy waved. "Mother!"

The Captain rushed down the ramp into his wife's arms. Next to her stood a younger woman similar in height, holding a baby wrapped in white linen. Beside them was another girl with the same brown hair as Lucy.

Lucy's pace picked up and soon they, too, were embraced by the group.

"Darling," the Captain said, bringing his wife's hand to his mouth, "I'd like to introduce you to the young man I wrote you about." The woman smiled.

"Christopher, this is my wife." Mrs. Hughes' blue eyes glistened with pooled up tears of joy.

"It is nice to meet you, Ma'am," Christopher said, bowing.

"It's nice to meet you, too."

"Thank you for saving Papa," said Elizabeth, Lucy's eldest sister, passing her mother the baby. "I'm Elizabeth, and this is Evelyn."

"And this," Mrs. Hughes announced holding the

gurgling infant in her arms for all to see, "is Charlotte."

Captain Hughes swept the child away, holding her above his head. "Ahh, my dear you have blessed me with another daughter. I could not be more pleased." The baby cooed and the Captain brought the infant to his chest.

Evelyn pinched Lucy's arm and pulled her from Christopher's side as they walked through the crowds. "He is very handsome," she whispered in her sister's ear as they linked arms.

"He is," Lucy agreed.

"Is he yours?"

Lucy snorted acting as if her sister said the most ridiculous thing she had ever heard. "No!"

"Then you have no romantic feelings for him whatsoever?" Elizabeth asked, joining Evelyn.

Lucy shook her head. "None at all."

Evelyn wrapped her hair around her finger. "Then would you mind if I liked him?"

Christopher looked over his shoulder searching for Lucy, smiling when their eyes locked. Lucy's heartbeat doubled.

"Stay away from him, Evelyn."

"So you're not indifferent, then," Evelyn said with a laugh.

"Leave her alone." Elizabeth said. "Everyone knows I am the most beautiful. He will surely fancy me." Elizabeth turned her head to the side with her nose in the air.

Lucy pushed away from her sisters and rejoined Christopher.

"What was that about?" he whispered when she caught up to him.

"You don't want to know."

Elizabeth and Evelyn giggled.

Christopher dropped his hand to his side and Lucy wove her fingers through his reassuringly. "Are you sure?"

Lucy took a deep breath. Her sisters would never understand their bond. "Positive."

An open carriage waited to carry them to the house a short distance away. The last carriage Christopher was in had delivered him to the orphanage. He shuddered when he thought of how different life would have been had he not crawled into the barrel of herring so many months ago.

Lucy felt his pace slow. "Are you okay?"

"Yes, just thinking."

The carriage turned through town then slowly meandered up a dirt path. Lush green lawns gave way to a pleasant two-story white plantation-style house with a red tile roof and whitewash walls. Large pink flowers climbed up the side of the covered veranda where an attractive elderly woman waited for their arrival.

"Is that Miss Heffelfinger?"

Lucy grinned. "How did you know?"

"Cookie talked about her in the galley. I think he favors her quite a bit."

Lucy's grin turned to laughter.

The kindly woman ushered them all inside and offered them something cold to drink. The house was open to the land. Flowers crept through open windows and the scent of jasmine filled the air. From the informal sitting room, Christopher could see the masts of the ships at anchor in the bay below.

Miss Heffelfinger showed Christopher to his room leaving him to rest before supper. He was thankful for the quiet. The afternoon had been exhausting. He had no belongings, thus nothing to unpack. To his surprise, when he opened the closet and looked in the dresser drawers, he found that someone had already filled them with clothes for him to wear.

A knock sounded on the door.

"Christopher?" Mrs. Hughes called.

"Yes, ma'am," Christopher answered and opened the door.

"I hope you will find everything you need. I took the liberty of shopping for you myself."

Christopher didn't know how to answer.

"My husband and Lucy have told me much about you. You are a very brave young man. I hope you'll consider staying with us for a while."

Christopher blushed. "Thank you."

"Supper is at seven."

Christopher bathed and then changed before heading to the open family rooms.

The Captain and his wife and daughters were already gathered waiting for him to join them.

Mrs. Hughes walked over to him first and adjusted his shirt, checking to make sure the sizes she had chosen were accurate. He would be growing quickly, she thought, so she would need to have some larger clothes made for him soon.

Lucy waited patiently at her mother's side as she fussed. Christopher looked into her deep brown eyes.

"Captain?" Christopher said, when Mrs. Hughes was finished.

"Yes," the Captain answered.

"I have an answer to your earlier question."

The Captain raised his brow. "Yes?"

"If it's still agreeable with you and Mrs. Hughes, I'd like to stay." The room stilled.

"We'd like that, too," he said, stepping forward to wrap Christopher in a warm embrace. "It will be nice to have another man around here for a change."

The room filled with laughter.

From the rafters above their heads, Leo watched. "Lesson Five," he said quietly. The corners of his whiskers pulled up into a mousy grin. "Family is the greatest treasure of all."

- The End -

ACKNOWLEDGEMENTS

ARRGH! could not have happened without the help of several wonderful people.

At times writing this book was almost a bigger adventure than what took place within its pages.

First and always I need to thank my family: my husband, daughters, father, and stepmother, without whom I would not be where I am today.

Then my publisher and her amazing team who truly got me to pick up a manuscript I had all but given up on and start the painful process of rewriting.

From start to finish *ARRGH!* has been a seven-year battle of swords, wills, patience, and persistence.

Kari and Michelle, you guys are the best; thank you for your belief in a little boy and his mouse!

Nathan and Henry, thank you for inspiring your mom to take on a pirate book!

Sally, your help with revisions was invaluable!

My close friends, Christy, Anna, Linda, and Kristy, you guys listened to countless plot twists and ideas without ever telling me to be quiet. We are SO celebrating with a very good bottle of champagne!

Our friends Denis and Elizabeth, who after a couple of bottles of wine in Healdsburg, CA helped me come up with the title **ARRGH!** I wish we saw you more; that was a great weekend.

The extremely talented M. S. Corley. Your artwork is amazing. I feel truly blessed that we got to work together on this project and hope we can do it again.

And to my readers, I hope you enjoy **ARRGH!** Your support means everything.

THANK YOU

For more books from this author, visiting information, and author events please visit Stacey at:

www.staceyrcampbell.com

You can also learn more about Stacey R. Campbell on:
Twitter: @staceyrcampbell
Facebook: authorstaceyrcampbell
Pinterest: srcampbellwrite
&
Goodreads: Stacey R Campbell

Nothing says you love a book like writing a review.
Let your voice be heard. Make an author's day!
Thank You

CPSIA information can be obtained at www.ICGtesting.com
Printed in the USA
LVOW11*2123250315

432066LV00006B/27/P